A Mysterious Warning

Stephanie opened the door to her room. She stopped halfway to her bed, which was beside the window. What was that on her bed?

As she got closer, she saw that a dried black rose was lying across her pillow. Underneath it was a small piece of white paper.

"What's that?" Darcy asked. "Did someone leave you a flower? Is it from Ian?" She stared at the black rose. "Oh, my gosh. It's dead."

"What does the note say?" Allie asked.

Stephanie carefully picked up the note. The paper felt thin and fragile. When she opened it, she saw only four words, written in elegant old-fashioned script:

I warned you.

Edwina

"This is so creepy, Stephanie!" Allie said. "You got a message from a ghost!"

FULL HOUSE™: Stephanie novels

Phone Call from a Flamingo
The Boy-Oh-Boy Next Door
Twin Troubles
Hip Hop Till You Drop
Here Comes the Brand-New Me
The Secret's Out
Daddy's Not-So-Little Girl
P.S. Friends Forever
Getting Even with the Flamingoes
The Dude of My Dreams
Back-to-School Cool
Picture Me Famous
Two-for-One Christmas Fun
The Big Fix-up Mix-up
Ten Ways to Wreck a Date
Wish Upon a VCR
Doubles or Nothing
Sugar and Spice Advice
Never Trust a Flamingo
The Truth About Boys
Crazy About the Future
My Secret Secret Admirer
Blue Ribbon Christmas
The Story on Older Boys
My Three Weeks as a Spy
No Business Like Show Business
Mail-Order Brother
To Cheat or Not to Cheat
Winning Is Everything
Hello Birthday, Good-bye Friend
The Art of Keeping Secrets
What Can You Grow on a Family Tree?
Girl Power

Club Stephanie:

Fun, Sun, and Flamingoes
Fireworks and Flamingoes
Flamingo Revenge
Too Many Flamingoes
Friend or Flamingo?
Flamingoes Overboard!
Five Flamingo Summer
Forget It, Flamingoes!
Flamingoes Forever?
Truth or Dare
Summertime Secrets
The Real Thing
Rumor Has It
Three's a Crowd
He's the One

Available from MINSTREL Books

FULL HOUSE™ CLUB

Stephanie

Three's a Crowd

Based on the hit Warner Bros. TV series

Kathy Clark

A Parachute Press Book

Published by POCKET BOOKS
New York London Toronto Sydney Singapore

A MINSTREL PAPERBACK *Original*

A Minstrel Book published by
POCKET BOOKS, a division of Simon & Schuster, Inc.
1230 Avenue of the Americas, New York, NY 10020

A PARACHUTE PRESS BOOK

For information address Pocket Books, 1230 Avenue of the Americas, New York, NY 10020

ISBN: 0-671-04207-6

First Minstrel Books printing October 2001

10 9 8 7 6 5 4 3 2 1

For information regarding special discounts for bulk purchases, please contact Simon & Schuster Special Sales at 1-800-456-6798 or business@simonandschuster.com

Printed in the U.S.A.

CHAPTER 1

"I still can't believe we're going to be living here for two weeks!" Stephanie Tanner said as she walked down the stairs to the first floor of Kent House. She ran a hand along the elegant handrail on the curving marble staircase. Stephanie was thrilled to be staying in the large London mansion with her student tour group. "It's like being in a palace."

"I agree," Allie Taylor said. Her green eyes sparkled as she smiled. Allie was one of Stephanie's best friends from home. "I've never stayed in a place that's this nice."

"There's no way this place is haunted. I don't believe the rumors," Darcy Powell said as she surveyed the paintings on the wall beside her. She stopped to fasten a tortoiseshell clip in her short black hair.

"Neither do I," Stephanie said. Just before they left Paris, their teachers had told them that Kent House had a reputation for being haunted. In fact, one of the British students staying in the house already claimed to have seen a ghost. Stephanie didn't believe it was true. "Although I could see a ghost wanting to live here, because who *wouldn't* want to?"

"We're going to have such a blast in London. I can just tell," Darcy said. She pushed up the sleeves of her blue shirt.

"Hey, do you guys think I look okay?" Allie quietly asked Stephanie and Darcy. The three were on their way to meet ten British students, with whom they'd be making a short film. The video exchange program was a project created by some of Stephanie's teachers at home in San Francisco. The trip included stays in France, England, and Italy. Besides Stephanie, Darcy, and Allie, there were seven other students from their school on the summer tour—three more girls and four boys. In each country they visited, they were making film documentaries with their host students.

"Allie, you look *marvelous,* darling," Darcy said in an exaggerated accent. The girls had stopped on a landing to examine a landscape painting. "Seriously. I love your new blouse."

"Well, she bought it in Paris, after all." Stephanie pushed her long blond hair behind her ears as she admired the pale green blouse that matched Allie's eyes. "So it *has* to look good. And wait until everyone back home sees it."

"Yeah, and wait until I tell my parents that I already spent *half* of my traveler's checks." Allie grimaced. "We'll be on this trip for a whole month more."

"Don't worry about money right now," Darcy said as the girls moved down the last stairs. "Just enjoy the fact that we're staying in a mansion. Because we're not going to get a chance like this again. This is a once-in-a-lifetime opportunity."

"Give me a break," Rene Salter said, waiting at the bottom of the stairs. "I don't know what you guys are making such a big deal about. This house is nothing compared to my uncle's ocean-side ranch in Carmel." She flipped her stylish shoulder-length brown hair so it rested on the shoulders of her designer sweatshirt.

"Oh, well. La-di-da." Darcy rolled her eyes.

"It's much bigger, plus it has a little deck off

each bedroom and a whirlpool and a sauna," Rene bragged.

Stephanie was used to Rene's superior attitude, but it still annoyed her. Rene was a member of a club called the Flamingoes that Stephanie had decided not to join back in the sixth grade. Rene *still* held it against her. She constantly competed with Stephanie, and she'd do anything to win any competition. To Stephanie Rene was impossible, but luckily Rene had two close friends on the summer trip: Tiffany Schroeder and Cynthia Hanson.

Stephanie followed Darcy out the French doors and onto the back terrace. The afternoon sun blinded her for a second, and she had to put a hand over her eyes to shield them. When she could see again, she nearly had her breath taken away by the view. "Wow! I've never seen so many flowers," she said, admiring the lush, elaborate garden. Hedges had been pruned into geometric shapes, and large trees bordered the wide green lawn that enclosed the flower beds.

On the terrace, students and teachers were sitting at wrought-iron tables. A linen cloth covered a table cluttered with plates of food, elegant glasses, and silver pitchers.

"Whoa," Rene said.

Stephanie could tell that even Rene was impressed by the garden.

"Don't look now," Allie whispered as she gazed at a couple of boys milling around the refreshment table. "But isn't that guy in a *band?* You know, he's the drummer in that Irish band with the four guys who dance and—"

"Are only the cutest guys in the entire world?" Stephanie added. She knew which student Allie was talking about. He was tall and thin, with shoulder-length dirty blond hair. He was wearing cool sunglasses, a retro T-shirt, and baggy jeans.

"Oh, you're right—he totally looks like Patrick from the Boggarts," Darcy agreed. "Except maybe five years younger."

"Too bad he isn't in the band," Allie said. "Then we could meet the rest of the Boggarts."

I think meeting him will be awesome enough, Stephanie thought as she watched the boy walk toward her.

"Hello there!" He came right up to Stephanie and held out his hand. "And who might you be?"

"I'm Stephanie," she said as they shook hands. Then she quickly introduced the other girls with her: Darcy, Allie, Rene, Cynthia, and Tiffany. The boys in their school group were sitting at a table with other British students.

"My name's Ian Thornton. And it's great to meet you," he said as he looked into Stephanie's eyes. Then he coughed and looked around. "I mean, it's great to meet all of you."

Stephanie smiled nervously. "You, too," she told him. Was it her imagination, or did he seem to like her?

"How was your flight?" Ian asked.

"Oh, we took the train," Stephanie said.

"From the States? I didn't know there was a train across the ocean," Ian said. "First the Chunnel, now this." He shook his head. "Man, the things they're doing with technology . . ."

Stephanie laughed. "Actually, we spent the last two weeks in Paris."

"A-ha." Ian nodded. "That explains it. And I have to admit, I'm rather jealous. Two weeks in Paris? How was it?" He grinned at Stephanie.

"Awesome," Stephanie said. *Unless you consider the fact I got completely blown off by Tristan, the guy I liked. Which I hope won't happen again.* Stephanie's crush on the resident adviser in their French dorm had ended in disaster because she helped him make a video at night. She had ended up breaking a camera and getting caught sneaking out after hours. "So, who else is here?" she asked Ian.

"Only the best film crew *this* side of the Atlantic," Ian said. "First we've got Sean, my best pal." He nodded to a shorter boy with dark brown skin and very short brown hair who had walked over to stand next to him. "And then there's Nigel, who knows more about movies than Alfred Hitchcock. He's like a walking encyclopedia of film trivia." Nigel moved over to them on cue.

"Actually, I prefer to think of myself as a director in training," Nigel said as he slid his tiny rectangular glasses up on his nose. "This will be the first of many films for me."

Stephanie glanced over at Corey Griffin, who had transferred to her school right before the trip. *Funny. Nigel sounds exactly like Corey,* she thought. *Maybe he and Nigel can hang out and discuss camera angles.*

Stephanie thought that Corey was really good-looking, with his short blond hair and intense blue eyes. He could be nice and funny, too, but even though they met only two weeks ago, they had already clashed several times. On their Paris video shoots, Corey wanted to be in charge—all the time. *And, to be honest, so did I,* Stephanie thought. They had finally managed to become friends on their last few days in Paris.

"Ah. And here's Vanessa now," Ian said. A tall, beautiful girl with shiny auburn hair walked over. She had a bottle of mineral water in one hand and a cookie in the other.

"Yes?" Vanessa said with a sweet smile.

"Vanessa Durrell, please meet Stephanie, and Darcy . . . and uh . . ." Ian faltered.

Darcy finished introducing everyone else. *At least he remembered my name,* Stephanie thought happily.

"It's great to meet all of you," Vanessa said. "Have you had any of these shortbreads yet? They're delicious. And they've got little jam tarts and sandwiches as well."

"I'd love to try some. I'm starving," Rene told her.

"Follow me," Vanessa said.

"Vanessa, hold on a second. Clare!" Ian called to a thin girl with long black hair walking past.

She jerked around with a startled expression. "What?" she asked breathlessly. "What's wrong?"

"It's just terrible, actually," Ian said.

"What?" Clare asked. "What is it?"

"Nothing," Vanessa said to Clare, who moved on. "Ian," Vanessa went on under her breath. "You really shouldn't tease her like that."

"I know," Ian said quietly. "But sometimes I just can't help myself." He winked at Stephanie, then leaned closer to her. "She's so easily spooked, you see. If you say 'Boo!' she passes out cold."

"Then I'll have to be careful," Stephanie said. "Hi, Clare," she called out to the shy girl. "I'm Stephanie," she said, introducing herself. "Don't worry, there's nothing wrong," she added when she saw the terror in Clare's eyes.

"Yes, don't let Ian scare you," Vanessa spoke up. "He really wouldn't hurt a fly."

Stephanie noticed Ian and Vanessa exchange an awkward glance as Clare moved up to the table and sat. She didn't have time to think much about it, because Mr. and Ms. Blith, two of Stephanie's teachers, called everyone together for a meeting. Ms. Blith introduced herself and her husband and then Mr. Hanley, the teacher who was supervising the English students. Then Mr. Hanley handed out sheets of information explaining the next two weeks' activities.

"We've taken the liberty of choosing topics for each team's video," Mr. Hanley said. "But if there are any objections, please speak up!"

Stephanie scanned the sheet of paper. The students had been divided into two teams, made up of both American and English students. Each team would make a video on a separate subject.

"Yes! We're on the same team again," Stephanie said to Darcy. She and Darcy would be on a team with Cynthia, Tiffany, Vanessa, Clare, Sean, Ian, and Corey. Their subject was "A Teen Tour of London's Hottest Spots."

Ian leaned over Stephanie's shoulder. "So what do you think of the topic?" he asked.

"It's, uh, great," Stephanie said, surprised at how close he was standing to her. *Especially our being on the same team!* she thought.

"Personally? I *love* it," Cynthia said. "Can we start tonight? I'm dying to go to a London club."

"Me, too," Darcy said.

"Did you guys come up with this topic?" Stephanie asked. "It's great."

"Yeah, we thought it might save time if we decided on these yesterday when we all got here and were kicking around ideas. If anyone doesn't like it, we could change it . . ." Ian paused.

Stephanie glanced over at Corey. He had strongly objected to their Paris video's topic at first, but it had turned out great in the end. Was he going to make a stink about this one, too?

"Well, Corey?" Stephanie finally asked. "What do you think? Will this make a good video?"

He smiled at her. "Sure," he said. "As long as we keep it interesting."

"Oh, don't worry about that," Ian said. "With me around? Things are always interesting." He winked at Stephanie.

This guy is too much, Stephanie thought. She hadn't met anyone so cocky and confident in a long time. And so far, she was definitely liking it!

London's going to be a lot different from Paris, she thought as Ian playfully read off a list of their upcoming shoots. *I can tell right now!*

"Well, Allie, we may not be on the same video team, but at least we get to share a room," Stephanie said as she unpacked before dinner that night.

Allie put a stack of T-shirts on top of a tall mahogany dresser. "I don't mind being in a different group. I think it'll be fun to work with Nigel."

"I love his name," Darcy said as she put her jacket on a hanger in the closet. "How come everyone's name here sounds so much cooler than ours?"

"Like Ian?" Stephanie said as she sat down on the elegant four-poster bed.

"Well, I wasn't *just* thinking of Ian, but I guess

you were." Darcy tossed a rolled-up pair of socks at Stephanie. "He totally likes you, you know."

"He does not—" Stephanie started to protest.

A loud, shrill shriek came from down the hallway. Stephanie jumped up and raced to the door.

"What was that?" Allie asked.

"I don't know—let's go find out!" Stephanie rushed down the hall toward the next bedroom as another scream pierced the air. Allie followed her, with Darcy right behind.

Stephanie skidded to a stop outside the bedroom that Tiffany, Cynthia, and Clare were sharing. Inside, Clare was edging toward the wall, her face pale.

"What is it?" Stephanie asked. "Clare, are you okay?"

"I—I saw her again!" Clare stammered.

"Saw who?" Stephanie put a hand on Clare's arm to comfort her.

Clare pointed to her bed. "She was there, right beside my bed. The ghost of Edwina Kent!"

CHAPTER 2

"So, Stephanie. Do *you* believe in ghosts?" Ian pulled out the chair next to Stephanie's at the dinner table that night. He sat down and gave her a broad smile.

Stephanie shook her head. She had been saving the seat for Allie, but she was psyched that Ian wanted to sit next to her. "No, I don't really go in for all that superstitious stuff," she told Ian.

"But you heard that Clare saw a ghost, right?" Ian asked. He snapped open a neatly folded cloth napkin and laid it across his lap.

"How could I not hear? She screamed so loudly!" Stephanie said. "We all ran to her room, and she was completely white," she added in a soft voice. She glanced down the table to where Clare was seated next to Mr. Hanley. "And she was totally convinced she saw this Edwina Kent person."

"It's the second time she's claimed she saw her," Nigel said from across the table. "She saw her the first day we arrived, before you got here."

"We heard about that," Cynthia Hanson said. "We were about to leave Paris, and Ms. Blith came running up to us. She told us this place was haunted. Needless to say, we couldn't *wait* to get here." She and Darcy laughed.

"Not me," Tiffany Schroeder said.

"I was being sarcastic, Tiffany," Cynthia said.

"Well." Tiffany did not look amused. "I think there should be some sort of team brought in to make sure there are no ghosts here. We have to live here for the next two weeks!"

"Sorry, Tiff. I don't think we actually *have* ghost busters here in England," Ian teased her.

"We might be able to find a bobby to come 'round and check the place out," Sean offered. "That's about it."

"Who's Bobby?" Tiffany asked.

Stephanie put a hand over her mouth to keep from laughing. Tiffany could be so funny sometimes, without meaning to be!

Beside her, Ian made no effort to hide his laughter. "Good one, Tiff!" he said.

"What?" Tiffany asked.

"Bobby's not a person," Rene explained. "It's what they call a police officer here."

"Well then, why don't they just *say* that?" Tiffany complained. She picked up her glass of water and took a sip.

"Because we have to be different," Ian said. He turned to Stephanie and smiled. "We *are* different, right?"

Stephanie smiled. "Definitely."

"Different strange? Or different . . . fascinating?" Ian asked.

Different cute, Stephanie thought, but she didn't get a chance to answer before Darcy spoke.

"So the question is, *could* there actually be a ghost haunting this place?" Darcy asked, taking in everyone at the table.

"Why not go straight to the source?" Ian said. "Mrs. Worthington? Would you help us with something, please?"

The housekeeper for Kent House stopped short as she set a large bread basket on the long table. "Yes, Ian? What is it now?" she asked with a sigh. "More cinnamon buns? I'm afraid you ate them all at breakfast."

"Oh, no—it's not about the food. And we don't mean to trouble you," Ian said. "But we were wondering—could you tell us the story behind the ghost here at Kent House?"

Mrs. Worthington dropped the butter dish with a clatter. "I'm not so sure that's a good idea, Ian."

"Please? I really want to hear the whole story," Allie said. "I know I won't be able to fall asleep tonight unless someone convinces me this *isn't* true."

"I'm afraid I can't do that," Mrs. Worthington said. She wiped her hands on her apron. "But if you must know the whole story . . . Well, there's our Edwina, right there." Mrs. Worthington pointed to a large portrait on the wall above the large stone fireplace in the formal dining room.

Stephanie stared at the painting. A finely dressed young woman with delicate features peered back at her with sad green eyes and a troubled expression. "Why isn't she smiling?" Stephanie asked. "Don't most people smile for their portraits?"

"Even Mona Lisa smiled a *little* bit," Ian joked.

"Edwina had a very hard life," Mrs. Worthington said.

"In this house? How could anyone have a hard life living in this beautiful place?" Darcy asked.

"Edwina Kent might have had all the material goods in the world," Mrs. Worthington said. "But that didn't keep her from getting her heart broken. That's why she looks so sad."

"So you think she knew what was coming?" Rene said.

"You mean she was psychic?" Tiffany asked.

"That might be true," Mrs. Worthington said. "Because that portrait was completed the day before she died."

"What?" Allie said, her voice shaky.

Stephanie felt a small chill go through her, too. She had spent at least ten minutes trying to convince Clare that there was no ghost haunting Kent House. Stephanie didn't believe in ghosts. Now, though, even *she* was starting to wonder.

"Come on, guys. Don't buy into this. I'm sure there's a perfectly logical explanation. How did she die?" Corey asked.

"That's just it. Nobody knows for certain," Mrs. Worthington said. "She was engaged to be married to a duke. They were supposedly very much in love. Everyone thought he was absolutely devoted to her, but it wasn't true. Edwina caught him kissing another girl. And that killed her."

"So wait a second. You're not trying to tell us

that she died of a broken heart?" Corey scoffed.

Mrs. Worthington acted offended. "And why not?"

Corey's just too practical! Stephanie thought. *He's not romantic at all.*

"The duke must have felt terrible," Cynthia said. "I'm surprised that his ghost isn't the one haunting the place. You know how they say spirits can't rest when they need to fix something in the past?"

"Obviously, this duke was a heartless chap," Sean said. "He didn't much care what he did."

"You've got a point," Darcy agreed.

"So, does anyone want to change their video idea now?" Ian asked. "To something about ghosts at Kent House?"

Everyone smiled.

"Hey, look on the bright side," Ian continued. "If this place wasn't haunted, we couldn't stay here at the discount ghost-in-every-room rate."

Mrs. Worthington shook her head as she tried not to laugh. "Now, if you'll excuse me, I'll be back with the rest of dinner in just a minute."

Stephanie sneaked a sideways glance at Ian. He was good-looking, funny, intelligent, and charming. If Stephanie wasn't careful, she was going to fall for him—if she hadn't already!

* * *

The next day Stephanie's team spent the morning storyboarding, planning each shot of their video. They chose each location and made a list of jobs for every team member. In the afternoon they met the other video team for a tour of the Tower of London. Stephanie had never seen such an amazing old fortress before. She was really enjoying walking around the Tower Green on their tour.

"You had the best ideas this morning," Stephanie told Vanessa, who walked beside her. "I can't wait to see the Doc Martens Super Store when we start shooting tomorrow," Stephanie added, referring to the famous shoe store.

"You'll love it. I have lived here most of my life," Vanessa said, "so I'd *better* come up with some decent ideas, right?" She pointed to a black bird sitting on a railing. "See that raven? It lives here. Its wings are clipped so it can't fly."

"Why's that?" Stephanie asked as she smiled at the bird.

"There's an old belief that when the ravens fly away from the Tower of London the kingdom of England will fall," Vanessa explained. "So all of their wings are clipped."

"It doesn't look very friendly," Stephanie commented.

"No, ravens aren't exactly chummy." Ian spoke up from behind Stephanie and Vanessa. "You know, it's too bad Clare didn't go for my idea—filming at Madame Tussaud's, the wax museum. I'd love to pose us near those wax figures, especially the ones in the Chamber of Horrors."

"Mmm," Vanessa said. "Well, Clare would faint before she even made it through the door."

"Probably," Stephanie agreed as she glanced back at Clare, who was walking between Ms. Blith and Mr. Hanley. Apparently, even the Tower of London frightened her. Stephanie could understand why—she had read in the brochure that many famous people in history had been imprisoned and died there. When Ian had suggested checking out the Bloody Tower, Clare had shrieked so loudly that one of the guards—known as Beefeaters—had come to see what was wrong!

"Hey, I was wondering something about our video," Corey said as he caught up to Vanessa, Stephanie, and Ian.

Stephanie turned to him. She half expected him to ask whether he could direct it all himself, even though they had already agreed to share the directing duties. She had to smile when she saw his cool Eiffel Tower T-shirt, which he had bought in Paris. The blue of the shirt really brought out the blue of his eyes.

"When we were in Paris, our video got shown on the evening news," Corey said directly to Vanessa. "What do you think? Could we pull that off here, too?"

"I don't see why not," Vanessa told him. "I mean, it might be difficult. But maybe if I called my parents, I could see if they have any connections."

"That would be really cool," Corey said. "You'd do that for me? I mean—for us?"

"Sure," Vanessa said with a shrug.

"I was wondering something else, too, Vanessa. Since you know the city so well," Corey said. "If we get some free time, could you show me where the Design Museum is? I really want to check it out." He ran a hand through his short blond hair.

"No problem, I'll take you on a tour. Anywhere you like!" Vanessa smiled at Corey. Her silver earrings glinted in the sun.

"You know what? You guys are great hosts," Corey said as he smiled at Vanessa.

Stephanie was a little taken aback. She wasn't absolutely sure, but she could swear that Corey was flirting with Vanessa. *What's going on? Does he have a crush on Vanessa or something?* she wondered.

"And here we are at the Bloody Tower," Mr. Hanley said. "This is where prisoners and traitors were locked up." He gave them a brief history of the way prisoners were brought in at night, on boats, through Traitor's Gate.

Ian took Stephanie's arms and playfully pretended to push her toward the Tower. "If we can just lock up Stephanie, we'd have one less person to deal with on this video!"

"Hey! Why me?" Stephanie laughed as she tried to fight back. She found herself standing so close to Ian, she could kiss him. She stared into his eyes, which were sparkling with amusement. "Oh, so it's funny to you," Stephanie said.

"Ian, stop it!" Clare said as she tugged on his arm. "Don't even *joke* about it, okay? They found *skeletons* in there."

"Relax!" Ian said as he let Stephanie go. "I was only joking around, trying to get a rise out of you. Come on, then." He linked an arm through one of Clare's. "I promise I won't push anyone into a tower, or a moat—"

"There's no water in the moat here anymore," Clare said.

"See? I *told* you I wouldn't do it," Ian said.

Stephanie laughed and was about to follow the two of them, when she spotted Vanessa and

Corey standing off to one side. Their heads were close together as they talked intently. It looked as if they had known each other for months, not just days. Stephanie felt a tiny twinge of jealousy as she watched them. She didn't know why she felt jealous—she didn't like Corey that way, even though she had felt attracted to him when they first met. Sure, Corey was really good-looking, and funny, and smart, but she didn't want to *date* him. Ian was more her type of guy, anyway.

So I don't get it, she thought. *Why does seeing Corey flirt with Vanessa bother me so much?*

CHAPTER 3

The next morning Stephanie stepped onto the subway train. Someone behind her pushed her forward as she boarded the car. When she grabbed for a pole to hang on to, her hand closed right on top of someone else's!

"Sorry!" Stephanie said as the person in front of her turned around.

It was Corey! Stephanie quickly moved her hand off his.

"No problem," Corey said.

"Um, is it okay if I hang on here, too?" Stephanie asked as the train started moving through the tunnel to Covent Garden and the Doc Martens store.

"Sure. Of course," Corey said as his face turned red.

Stephanie knew exactly how he felt. She was embarrassed, too! "So, uh, this is the tube," she said awkwardly.

Corey nodded. "Yes, it is." He smiled at her.

"Why aren't we filming down here?" Stephanie asked. "This is definitely a hot spot. Right? I mean, there are like hundreds of teens on this train. Not counting us."

"I've always wanted to make an underground film," Corey joked. "You know what would be cool? Filming from the first car as we barrel through the tunnel."

"That's a great idea!" Stephanie said. "We could do that. You know what I'd like to do? I'd love to add little subtitles to our video. So we could sort of do a running narration."

"Like Pop-up Video?" Corey asked. "You can insert titles if you learn how to use the Print Shop program. I know it. I could teach you," he offered.

"Would you? That would be awesome," Stephanie told him.

"Yeah, well, I know you're a pretty fast learner," Corey said. "I saw your editing work in Paris, remember?"

Stephanie nearly fell over—and it wasn't from

the train's stopping. Was Corey actually complimenting her? "So, do you have any ideas for funny titles? I mean, I know it's a little early, since we haven't *shot* any scenes yet, but—"

"Let's see. I think I do have a couple of lines. What do you think of these?"

As Corey mentioned his ideas, Stephanie struggled to pull out a small notebook to write them down, not believing how well they were getting along. The train had stopped at a few stations and let off several passengers, so it wasn't nearly as crowded. There were even empty seats. But neither Corey nor Stephanie made a move for them. They obviously both wanted to keep talking.

About five minutes later Rene, whose group was also going to Covent Garden, suddenly rushed up to them. "Corey, did you see my pack?" she asked.

"Your what?" Corey turned toward her.

"My little pink backpack!" Rene was desperate. "I had it when we got on the tube, and now it's gone."

"Are you sure you didn't just put it down somewhere?" Stephanie asked.

"I put it on the seat beside me," Rene said. "Someone must have stolen it. The train was so crowded. Now what am I going to do?

Everything important I have was in there—everything!" Rene grabbed Corey by the arm as the train lurched.

"Don't panic," Corey said. "We'll figure out what to do. Come on, let's go talk to Ms. Blith."

Stephanie watched them go, feeling a little irritated. It wasn't that she didn't feel sorry for Rene if she truly had lost her backpack. It was just that she and Corey had been having a great conversation—their first real talk since that night they'd edited their video in Paris. Stephanie was completely enjoying it, and she hated being interrupted.

She frowned as she watched Rene ask Mr. and Ms. Blith what she should do. Rene losing something didn't make sense. That was more like something Tiffany would do. *Did she make it up just so she could pull Corey away from me?* Stephanie wondered.

"All right, kids—this is us," Mr. Hanley said as the tube slowed at the next stop. "Everyone out! Get your things!"

Stephanie saw Nigel and Sean lift up the camera equipment near their feet. Nigel pulled out a camera bag.

"A-ha!" Ian was sitting across the train from them and he leapt to his feet. He pulled out a small pink backpack from underneath the seat just as the doors opened at their stop. "What's this, then? Is this what you were going on about, Rene?"

"Yes! You found it!" Rene cried as everyone spilled out onto the platform. "Ian, you're a life saver."

Stephanie shook her head. "Maybe next time you should actually look around *your* seat," she told Rene as she walked past.

"I did," Rene insisted. "Ian, I can't thank you enough. I'd completely given up. And you have no idea how important this bag is to me."

"Well, then. I'm not sure I'm going to give it back," Ian teased as he held it behind his back. "What have you got in here? Cash? Stocks? No, wait—it's a diary, isn't it? I bet that's some juicy reading."

"Stop it!" Rene said with a laugh as she lunged for the pack.

"Okay, here you go. But take a tip from me—wear it on your back from now on," Ian said. "That way you won't lose it again. And don't leave any of the pockets open when you're on the tube. Someone could lift something out of it. All right?"

Rene nodded as she smiled and looped the

straps over her shoulders. "I'm never taking this off again, Ian."

"Fine by me, but it's not going to be very comfortable sleeping," Ian joked.

"Thanks for helping me look for it, anyway," Rene told Corey as they headed up the stairs side by side.

"No problem," Corey said politely. "Anytime."

"Well, Stephanie, are you ready to see Covent Garden?" Ian did an elaborate bow. "After you, Mademoiselle Tanner. That *is* what all the hip French guys called you, right?"

"Oh, um, sure," Stephanie said, distracted by watching Corey and Rene. Was Rene interested in Corey, too? *And why do I care, when I have a cute guy like Ian waiting for me?*

"Check these out!" Darcy rushed up to Stephanie carrying a pair of neon blue shoes. "You can't get these Docs at home. Aren't they the coolest?"

"This store is so great," Allie said. She looked up at the flashing strobe light overhead. "It's like being in a dance club or something."

"I love those shoes," Stephanie told Darcy. "Do they have your size?"

"I don't know, but I'm about to find out. Come

on, Allie, help me get a salesclerk." Darcy tugged Allie's sleeve and started to drag her away.

"Hey, Darcy? We need to set up the camera!" Corey called her. "We're here to film other people buying shoes—remember?"

Darcy set down the camera bag next to Corey. "You guys get started—I'll be *right* back." She took off with Allie.

"Sure she will," Stephanie said. "Just as soon as she tries on every shoe here."

Corey laughed. "I can't blame her. I was actually thinking of checking out the shoes today, then coming back tomorrow with my traveler's checks."

"Sounds like a great idea. Well, Darcy is a teen. And this is a hot spot," Stephanie said. "Do you want to start by filming her?"

"How about if we wait a few minutes? After everyone's had a chance to check out the place, we might be able to concentrate a bit better," Vanessa said.

"You're probably right. That sounds like a good idea," Corey told her.

Stephanie noticed that *whatever* Vanessa said seemed like a good idea to Corey. He was completely infatuated with her.

"Come on, you two—did you see the customized shoes?" Vanessa asked as she led them to a large display. Corey followed closely behind her. "Look, they're all signed by different celebs."

"Wow," Stephanie said as she admired a pair that had been signed by Lauryn Hill.

"No doubt these are very fascinating," Ian commented. "Especially those!" He pointed to a pair of shoes signed by the band No Doubt.

"Ha-ha." Stephanie punched him lightly on the arm. "Very funny."

"My favorites are those. The ones signed by the Boggarts!" Cynthia said.

"Mine, too." Vanessa sighed. "They're my absolute favorite band in the world."

"I love the Boggarts, too," Stephanie agreed. "Are they as popular here as they are back home in the States?"

"Even more! Guess what? I heard they're going to be in London for the next two weeks, shooting a video," Vanessa said. "I hope we have a chance of running into them."

"If they hang out at any of the hot spots we're filming, we'll see them," Sean said. "But I bet they can't do tourist things without fans mobbing them."

"Fans like me, you mean," Vanessa said. "I'd mob them in a second."

"I'd probably knock someone down just to get an autograph," Stephanie admitted.

"Stephanie, I think you're more impressed by that singer chap's shoes than you are by me." Ian sat on the steps to the next level of the store and rested his chin in his hands.

"What?" Stephanie asked with a laugh.

"No, it's obvious. You're obsessed with the Boggarts, just like every other girl on the planet," Ian said.

"I don't think I'd call it obsessed," Stephanie said. "Anyway, you look like one of the guys in the band. Doesn't that help? If we like him, then we must like you—right?"

"I don't know, Stephanie. It's just . . . I can't help feeling your heart's already devoted to someone else," Ian said.

"What? No, it isn't," Stephanie said. Her lively conversations with Corey popped into her mind, but she pushed them away. Corey only seemed to have eyes for Vanessa.

"Good." Ian gave her a wink. "If I get a new pair of Docs, maybe I'll have a chance, too." He wandered off toward the shoe racks.

A few minutes later Darcy came up to

Stephanie with her new purchase in her hands. "I was just talking to Ian, and one thing's obvious, Steph," she said. "Ian definitely likes you—a lot! So the question is, do you like him?"

"I definitely like Ian. He's great," Stephanie said just as Corey had appeared at her side. He looked away, and Stephanie felt her face turn pink. It was so embarrassing to be caught gushing over Ian! Especially after the way she had fallen for Tristan, their R.A. back in Paris—which Corey knew all about!

Why does saying I like Ian in front of Corey feel so weird? Stephanie wondered.

CHAPTER 4

"Mrs. Worthington is an incredible cook, isn't she?" Allie said that night as she, Stephanie, and Darcy walked down the hall from the large, formal dining room.

"I don't think she does *all* the work," Stephanie said. "She has a huge staff helping her, including a chef, a butler—"

"And a dishwasher, I hope," Darcy said. "Didn't we each use about ten plates?"

Stephanie was about to count off the different courses they'd had for dinner, when she heard laughter coming from one of the drawing rooms down the hall.

"That sounds like Cynthia," Darcy said. "Let's go see what she's up to."

Stephanie followed Darcy toward the open doorway. Inside, Cynthia, Tiffany, Clare, Vanessa, and Rene were sitting at a round mahogany card table. Rene and Vanessa were leaning toward each other, speaking privately.

"Rene and Vanessa seem like they've become best friends," Stephanie commented.

"No kidding. Check out Vanessa's shirt," Darcy said. "It's as pink as that dumb backpack Rene almost lost. What is she, an honorary Flamingo or something?"

"She could be president of the London chapter," Stephanie joked. *Just what the world needs—a British Flamingo. Someone else for Rene to order around!* She, Allie, and Darcy entered the drawing room.

"Hi, guys. What's up?" Darcy asked. She took a seat on the dark green velveteen sofa beside the card table. Allie sat next to her, while Stephanie pulled up a chair.

"Not much," Cynthia said. "We're just watching Vanessa's amazing card tricks."

"What's amazing is that she doesn't actually know any," Clare said with a giggle. "She just keeps pretending she does!"

"Hey, I'm not that bad," Vanessa said. "Didn't

I tell you your card was the queen of hearts?"

"Yes, and you were dead wrong," Clare said. "Remember? It was the three of diamonds."

Everyone started laughing again.

"Oh, well. I suppose I have a bit of work to do." Vanessa scratched her arm.

"Hey, if you guys want to play a game, I'm in," Stephanie said.

Vanessa shuffled the deck of cards. "Actually, speaking of games . . . Rene and I were talking earlier, and we thought of the perfect way to find out more about Edwina Kent," she said.

"Go to the library?" Darcy asked.

"No, this will be a lot more fun than doing boring research," Rene said. "We're going to try to communicate with Edwina—directly."

Cynthia folded her arms across her chest. "And how exactly are you going to do that?" She sounded very skeptical.

"Wait for her ghost to show up and scare me to death again?" Clare asked.

"No, of course not," Vanessa said. "We wouldn't want that, silly. In fact, we were thinking maybe we could communicate with her and tell her *not* to scare you anymore."

"Check out what we found hiding in this

chest." Rene opened the top and pulled out what looked like a board game.

Then Stephanie recognized the box. "A Ouija board?"

"Isn't it great?" Rene opened the box and took out the board. She set it on the table. "Everyone in?"

"Uh, I don't know," Tiffany said. "Those things give me the creeps."

"Come on, Tiffany. There's nothing to be afraid of," Rene said. "Right, Cynthia?"

"It's just a game," Cynthia said. "Remember when we used it to find out which boys liked us?"

Tiffany smiled. "Oh, yeah. That *was* fun."

"Well, we can have fun tonight," Rene declared. "We can see if Edwina Kent answers us. It could be a real séance!"

"Let's dim the lamps and light some more candles," Vanessa suggested.

Everyone was gathered around the table a few minutes later. Stephanie had to admit that the room looked right for a séance: dimly lit, a little eerie—and it was even raining outside!

"I'm not sure I should be here," Clare said. "Maybe I'll go upstairs."

"Clare, don't be silly." Vanessa reached across the table and put a hand over one of Clare's.

"We're all here together. Nothing scary is going to happen."

"Besides," Darcy said. "If you went upstairs, you'd be all alone, because *we'd* still be down here."

Clare bit her lip and seemed to be even more nervous. "Good point. Okay, let's get this thing started," she said. "But let's ask only *fun* questions!"

Everyone put her fingers on the edge of the small white plastic triangle that would move around the board. Stephanie remembered that it was called a planchette. She hadn't used a Ouija board in a long time, though, and she had forgotten how much fun it could be.

"All right. Our first question is . . . Edwina, are you there?" Vanessa asked.

Stephanie waited for the planchette to move. Nothing happened.

"She's not answering," Clare said. "Okay, well, let's pack it in—"

"Not so fast. We have to try a few times," Rene told her. "Edwina, if you're there," she said, "please spell out 'Hello.'"

Stephanie gasped as the planchette started to move. Her eyes stared at the board as it drifted from one letter of the alphabet to another: *R, X, I, U, L.*

"She's a really horrible speller," Darcy joked.

"That's one little fact about Edwina Kent that's not well known."

Allie giggled. "So much for our séance!"

"Hey, maybe she's just getting warmed up," Stephanie joked.

"Come on, everyone, concentrate—really, really hard," Vanessa urged. "Edwina, if you're here, please let us know. Send us a message. Who do you have a message for?"

There was a pause, and then Stephanie felt the planchette begin to move again. This time it landed on the letters S and T.

"ST?" Rene asked. "What's that?"

"Me," Stephanie said. "I mean, my initials are S.T. Are anyone else's?" She looked around the circle of girls hopefully. She didn't know why, but she didn't want a message right now—especially from a ghost!

"Look, it's moving again!" Allie said.

Stephanie watched and waited as the planchette spelled out the following sentence: *Guard your heart.*

"What's that supposed to mean?" Tiffany asked. "Are you going to have a heart attack or something?"

The planchette kept moving. *Beware of romance. Ignore me at your peril!*

Stephanie stared at the board when the planchette stopped. Was it going to move again? Was the message over? She held her breath in anticipation.

After a minute of silence everyone released the planchette. Then Stephanie felt all eyes turn to her.

"Stephanie, that message was for you," Allie said. "It's a warning from Edwina Kent!"

CHAPTER 5

"She's right," Clare said. "Edwina died of a broken heart, remember? Now she's trying to make sure that no one else is in the same danger. Stephanie, she was warning you."

Stephanie shook her head. "It doesn't make sense. My heart isn't broken," she pointed out. "It isn't going to be broken, because I'm not in love. In fact, I'm not even close." She did have a little crush on Ian, but it wasn't that serious. Besides, she'd never admit liking anyone in front of Rene.

"Not *yet,*" Allie said. "But if you were in love—"

"But I'm not," Stephanie argued. "So the message doesn't make any sense. Besides, it wasn't from Edwina. It couldn't have been."

"I don't know," Allie said slowly. "I'm not so sure."

"Neither am I," Clare added. "It sounds exactly like something Edwina's ghost would say."

"And we can't prove she *didn't* say it," Tiffany observed. "Ooh. I can't believe we're living in a creepy haunted house. I want my money back."

"Who cares about that?" Clare said. "I'm too scared to go to sleep tonight. If she comes back . . ."

"She won't come back," Stephanie said firmly.

"How do you know?" Vanessa asked. "I say she's going to watch our every move until we leave."

"I agree. She obviously knows everything that's going on in this house. And she *doesn't* want us here," Clare said.

"She didn't say that," Stephanie interrupted. "Even if she did try to communicate with us, she was only trying to warn us so that our hearts wouldn't be broken."

"So that *your* heart wouldn't be broken," Vanessa reminded Stephanie. "Your initials were on the board, Stephanie. No one else's."

Vanessa sounded so serious that Stephanie felt uneasy. She quickly pushed her fears aside. "A lot of people in the world have my initials," Stephanie joked. "The message could have been for anyone else."

"But we were having a séance here, in her house, and the point of a séance is for the spirit to contact *us.*" Rene folded up the board and put it back into the box. "Face it, Stephanie. Edwina Kent was talking to you. And if I were you, I'd steer clear of any romances for the next few weeks."

"Yeah, remember what happened to Edwina," Clare said.

Stephanie looked up at a small portrait of Edwina that hung on the drawing room wall. Was she trying to communicate with Stephanie? And if so, why?

I'm not in danger of losing my heart—to anyone, Stephanie thought, determined. *Am I?*

A little later they all went upstairs to bed. Allie closed the door to their bedroom, while Darcy opened a window for some fresh air. Stephanie reached into the top drawer of her dresser to pull out her nightshirt.

"Well, I don't know what that Ouija board message means, or if it means anything." Darcy paused beside Stephanie's bed. "But could you do me a favor?"

"Sure," Stephanie said. "What is it?"

"Just promise me something, Steph. Just be careful, okay?" Darcy said. "Be really careful."

Stephanie looked at Darcy's worried face. This was supposed to be a fun trip, and it had definitely started out that way. So why did everyone have to get so freaked out over a nonexistent person? And why did the Ouija board have to warn her, of all people?

"Wait a second. I thought our tour was of hot spots." Ian rubbed his bare arms. "We're in an ancient *crypt*. A tomb. And it's freezing in here!"

"Do you think they sell sweaters in the bookshop?" Stephanie asked with a laugh.

She was really enjoying their visit to the Café-in-the-Crypt. It was located inside an old church called St. Martin-in-the-Fields, which had served London in many ways over the years. Famous people were buried inside the crypt. From 1914 to 1927 it had served as a shelter for poor and homeless citizens. And finally, during the Second World War, it had been used as an air raid shelter, a place to hide out from the massive bombing raids on the city.

It still served as a church, a place for concerts, and a soup kitchen for the homeless. In addition, there was the Café-in-the-Crypt, a bookshop, and the London Brass Rubbing Center.

"Hello, mate! Are we filming yet?" Sean walked over to Ian.

Vanessa trailed behind him, and she stopped next to one of the giant stone pillars. "Where did everyone go?" she asked.

"They must be trapped in the crypt," Ian said.

"Agggghhhhh," Sean screamed. "I'm trapped, I'm dying, help me . . ."

"Really. You are too much," Vanessa said in a bored tone.

"Can you imagine the people who are buried here? I mean, talk about not letting your spirit rest," Ian said. "You've got people trampling all over your burial ground, drinking caffè lattes and eating cookies. Very disrespectful, if you ask me."

"How'd you like to have crumbs on your grave site?" Sean said. "I can just imagine the old coots in there. 'If those people would stop walking around, I might get a decent night's sleep,'" he said as he imitated an older man's voice.

"I'm so sick of smelling coffee, I could just die," Ian joked. "Wait a second. I *am* dead."

"You're dead? Look at me. I haven't been this

pale since the cold front of 1721," Sean said.

"Ah, that was a nasty one, all right," Ian said. "It almost killed me." He and Sean cracked up.

Vanessa glanced at Stephanie and rolled her eyes. "They actually think they're *funny.*"

A small smile curled up at the corners of Stephanie's mouth. She didn't say anything, but she thought Ian and Sean were hilarious. And she loved the way Ian was always trying to entertain her.

"I'll go find the others," Vanessa said with a sigh.

"Let me come along," Sean offered. "That way I can save you from the crazy old ghosts in here."

"And we'll stay here," Ian said once they were gone. He walked over to Stephanie with a smile. "Can you believe it? We're actually alone. I thought that wasn't allowed on this tour." He reached for Stephanie's hands. "Come on, let's get out of here while we still can." He started to pull her toward the side door.

"But we can't just *leave!*" Stephanie protested as Ian gripped her hands tighter. She leaned back, trying to drag her feet.

"Oh. We can't?" Ian stopped dead in his tracks, and Stephanie crashed into him. "Well, then. I suppose we'll have to do this here."

Stephanie felt her heart beat faster as Ian pulled her even closer. He lowered his face to hers, and their lips met in a soft kiss.

Stephanie felt a shiver go down her spine, but she wasn't sure if it was from Ian's kiss—or from being kissed in a crypt. Something about it sort of gave her the creeps.

Don't be ridiculous, she told herself. *This incredibly fun and wonderful guy just kissed you!*

"Ahem!" Somebody behind them cleared his throat.

"Ignore that." Ian brushed a strand of Stephanie's long blond hair off her cheek. "Probably one of those old coots, upset that we're kissing while they're still dead."

Stephanie giggled.

"Excuse me," a familiar voice said.

Oh, no, Stephanie thought. *That's Corey!* She pulled away from Ian.

"Mr. Hanley's wondering where you guys are. We're supposed to be shooting right now," Corey said awkwardly.

Stephanie turned around and saw Corey and Vanessa standing behind them. Neither one seemed very happy to have caught Ian and Stephanie locked in an embrace.

Corey was frowning at Stephanie, but he

wouldn't look her in the eye. Stephanie felt very embarrassed all of a sudden. Had they seen the whole thing?

"All right, then," Ian said. "Let's go film 'Tales from the Crypt, Version 2001'!"

Stephanie followed him. As she passed Corey, she tried to smile at him, but he wouldn't even look at her. *What's his problem?* she wondered.

That night, after going out for a dinner of fish and chips, everyone decided to turn in early. Stephanie, Darcy, and Allie headed to their bedroom upstairs.

"I can't wait to curl up in bed with my book," Allie said.

"I need to write a letter home," Darcy said. "My parents insisted on one long letter from each place we visit." She opened the door to their room.

"At least this one won't have to be in French!" Stephanie said. "Me, I can't wait to go to sleep—" She stopped halfway to her bed, which was beside the window. What was that on her bed?

As she got closer, she saw that a dried black rose was lying across her pillow. Underneath it was a small piece of white paper.

"What's that?" Darcy asked. "Did someone leave you a flower? Is it from Ian?" She stared at the black rose. "Oh, my gosh. It's *dead.*"

"What does the note say?" Allie asked.

Stephanie carefully picked up the note. The paper felt thin and fragile. When she opened it, she saw only four words, written in elegant old-fashioned script:

I warned you.
Edwina

CHAPTER 6

"That is so creepy!" Allie said as she stared at the black rose. "A ghost left you a *dead rose,* Stephanie."

"No, it's not from Edwina. Since when can ghosts write notes?" Stephanie placed the scrap of paper on top of her dressing table and faced Darcy and Allie. She wasn't going to let this get to her. It was silly. There was no way a ghost could be communicating with her—it was impossible! She had a feeling a certain Flamingo named Rene might be the one trying to get to her instead.

"You know what? The Ouija board was Rene's idea. I bet this note was written by Rene, too,"

Stephanie said. "That's why all this stuff is happening to me. It's Rene!"

"Do you really think so?" Allie asked. "I suppose it could be true, except . . . Clare really did think she saw Edwina's ghost, and Rene couldn't have pulled *that* off."

"Steph, normally I wouldn't put anything past Rene." Darcy picked up the note and studied it. "But I don't think her handwriting is this good. She doesn't know how to do fancy calligraphy."

"So she got someone to help her," Stephanie said. She grabbed the note from Darcy. "I'm going to rip this up and throw it away. This is all so stupid."

"Don't!" Darcy said. "Save it—as a handwriting sample."

Stephanie shoved the note into her top dresser drawer. "Okay. Now, how do I find out who can do fancy writing like that?"

"Call Scotland Yard?" Allie suggested. "Where's Sherlock Holmes when you need him?"

"What we need to do is get a sample of everyone's handwriting," Darcy said. "Then we can compare their writing to the note's. But how are we going to do that?"

"I've got it," Stephanie said. "Remember how

Ms. Donato said she wouldn't be around on Saturday because it's her birthday? And she had plans to get together with friends in London? Well, all I have to do is buy her a birthday card tomorrow, and ask everyone to sign it."

"Brilliant, Watson," Allie said. "Then you'll find out for sure if anyone here wrote this note—or if Edwina did."

"I just wish I could find out tonight," Stephanie said. "I don't know if I'm going to be able to sleep now."

"Sure you will," Darcy said. "Just think of you and Ian kissing," she teased Stephanie.

"Great." Stephanie tossed her barrette at Darcy. "Now I'll never fall asleep!"

The next day Stephanie's film crew returned to Covent Garden. Since visiting the Doc Martens store, they'd wanted to explore the area further.

"I love this place!" Darcy said enthusiastically as they walked up from the tube station. "Do you think I could convince my parents to move to London?"

Stephanie hoisted the tripod on her shoulder as she looked around the crowded square. It was an old open-air market that had been converted into shops and cafes. Street entertainers—musicians, jugglers, and comedians—roamed around to perform for the large crowd.

"First you have to convince my dad to let me move here," Stephanie replied. "Because no way are you living here without me."

"What's this? You girls are moving to London?" Ian jogged up beside them. "Excellent news." He winked at Stephanie. "Make sure you move to my neighborhood."

"You're not really moving here," Vanessa said. "Are you?"

Stephanie shook her head. "My dad would never go for it. He's got his own local TV show in San Francisco, so—"

"I absolutely adore San Francisco," Vanessa said. "In fact, Rene and I are already planning my visit. I hope I'll see you guys when I'm there!"

I don't know why you wouldn't, Stephanie thought. *Since wherever we go, Rene always ends up following us!*

"Okay, guys—this is a good place to set up our camera," Ian said. "We have a nice view of people coming and going. We can catch some of the strolling performers. We can interview people that go by. Teenagers like us, of course."

"And look—there's a karaoke stall, right in

front of us," Tiffany said excitedly. "That should be really entertaining!"

"Check out who's up there now," Cynthia said to Darcy. They laughed as an older woman belted out a Spice Girls song. A man with an Italian accent went next. He chose a Frank Sinatra song from the 1950s.

"Well, this won't do at all. We want footage of teens," Ian said. He started heading for the small stage, then turned around. "Stephanie, aren't you coming with me?"

"What?" Stephanie asked, flustered. She was helping Corey mount the camera on the tripod.

"I thought we could sing a duet," Ian said.

"Um, I'm sort of—I mean, I'm extremely busy," Stephanie said. *Besides, I'm terrible at karaoke—and if there's any chance this will be on film, forget it!*

"All right, then. I'll go solo," Ian said.

"Did you ever notice that Ian spends more time performing *for* the camera than actually standing behind it and filming?" Corey complained.

"But that's Ian," Sean said as he fitted a lens filter onto the camera. "And besides, we do need someone to ham it up now and again."

"True," Cynthia said as the music for a romantic ballad sung by Madonna started up.

Stephanie laughed. "He's not going to sing to this!"

"He is," Sean said. "Watch!"

"I'd rather not," Corey grumbled.

Stephanie had to agree with Corey on some level. Part of her wanted to ignore Ian—he was being completely silly. But part of her thought he was so charming, she couldn't look away.

"This one goes out to Stephanie," Ian said. "And she knows who she is. And so do all those other people standing right over there." He pointed to their film crew.

"This is so embarrassing! I'm glad we're the only people here with a video camera," Darcy said as she tried to hide behind it.

Stephanie cringed. Was he really going to sing an entire song to her—in the middle of one of London's most popular spots? *Allie's not going to believe this when we tell her.* I *don't believe this!*

"Look at it this way," Sean said to Darcy. "We're getting the footage we need, right?"

"That depends," Darcy said. "Are we making a 'London Bloopers' tape in addition to our other documentary?"

Sean laughed. "Are you saying Ian belongs in the not-so-hot spots flick?"

Stephanie blushed as Ian crouched down on bended knee to sing to her.

"Either that or the cutting room floor," Corey said as he frowned at Ian.

I don't care what Corey or anyone says, Stephanie decided as she grinned at Ian. *This might be goofy—but it's really romantic!*

"Do you think Ms. Donato will like her birthday card?" Stephanie asked Darcy as they walked out of a small shop later that afternoon.

Stephanie had spent at least fifteen minutes trying to pick out a card. Then Darcy had made her hurry and grab one, since they needed to meet the rest of the crew at four to head back to Kent House. They'd split up so that everyone could explore the area—half the group went with Mr. Hanley, the other half with Ms. Donato.

"I'm sure she'll be thrilled to get any card from all of us," Darcy said. "When will you get everyone to sign it?"

"Tonight, before dinner," Stephanie said. She couldn't wait to see who was behind her threatening note from "Edwina." She'd have to ask them all to sign the card in their best handwriting, though, if she wanted to get a clue from their signatures. Whoever had left her the scary note obviously wouldn't want to be caught. She'd have to study the signatures very carefully before turning the card over to Ms. Donato for her birthday.

"All set, girls?" Mr. Hanley asked. He had been shopping with the others in a store next door.

"Yes, thank you," Stephanie told him.

"I don't know what you had to do in secret, Stephanie," Ian said. "But I hope it was a gift for yours truly."

"Um . . ." Stephanie smiled at him. "Don't get your hopes up too high."

"It's for me, then," Sean declared as they started walking toward the fountain where they'd agreed to meet Ms. Donato. "Really, Darce. You shouldn't have."

"Good, because I didn't," Darcy said, laughing.

A few minutes later, before they reached the fountain, Darcy tugged at Stephanie's jacket sleeve.

"Look, isn't that Vanessa? With Corey?" Darcy asked. She gestured to a small flower garden off to the side, where Vanessa and Corey were perched on the stone wall surrounding it. They were sitting about fifty feet away from the fountain.

Vanessa was sitting with her back to Corey. Stephanie's eyes widened as Corey took what looked like a silver necklace out of a paper bag and fastened it around Vanessa's neck. *He's actually giving her jewelry now?* Stephanie thought. *Things between them are a lot more serious than I realized.*

Once Corey had fastened the clasp, Vanessa turned around—and gave Corey a big kiss!

Stephanie couldn't believe her eyes. Vanessa and Corey were a real couple now. *I know I should be happy for Corey,* Stephanie thought. *But I'm not!*

CHAPTER 7

"Stephanie! What are you doing?" Cynthia asked. She came up behind Stephanie, who was on her way up the stairs.

"I was just going to get something from my bedroom," Stephanie said as she paused. "Why?"

"Oh. Well, I thought we were all supposed to meet in the drawing room before dinner," Cynthia said. "That's what Darcy said."

"Right. And that's why I'm going to my room," Stephanie said. She lowered her voice. "We got a card today—for Ms. Donato's birthday on Saturday. And I want everyone to sign it."

"Wow," Cynthia said. "That's really thoughtful of you guys."

Sure it is, Stephanie thought as she slipped into her bedroom. *Except that we're using Ms. Donato's card as our opportunity to get a handwriting sample from everyone.* She grabbed the birthday card from the bag on her bed.

"Wait up—I was just coming up to grab a sweater," Cynthia said as she ducked into her bedroom. "I can't believe how cold and drafty this place gets. And it's *summer.*"

"I know. I think I figured out why they have fireplaces in nearly every room!" Stephanie said. "Now, if they'd just light them all, we'd be set."

"True. So how's Ian?" Cynthia asked as they headed for the stairs. "That was so funny today when he was singing to you. And what about Corey and Vanessa? Did you see them kissing?"

Stephanie nodded. *Did I ever!* she thought. She still didn't know why it had bugged her so much.

"This place is turning out to be way more romantic than Paris, don't you think?" Cynthia asked. "I can totally see you and Ian together. But Corey and Vanessa?"

"I don't know about that, either," Stephanie said. Vanessa was the last type of person she pictured Corey dating. But she had such mixed feelings when it came to Corey sometimes, she didn't trust her own reactions. Sometimes he was rude and obnoxious—other times he was sweet and nice. *If only he weren't so cute, maybe I wouldn't care so much!* Stephanie thought. She'd been attracted to Corey ever since the first time they met, back at the San Francisco airport. "Seeing Vanessa kiss him was sort of a shock," she confessed to Cynthia.

"To me, too! But then Rene was talking about it, and she pointed out that they look *so* great together. They're made for each other, Rene had said. It's so romantic," Cynthia concluded.

Stephanie thought of how she'd watched Vanessa kiss Corey. Then all the way back to Kent House on the tube, Vanessa and Corey had been sitting together, deep in conversation. It was all making Stephanie feel really uncomfortable.

But Ian kissed you, and you didn't object, Stephanie thought. *And you like Ian. So what's the big deal about Vanessa kissing Corey?*

Stephanie didn't know. All she knew was that Corey and Vanessa didn't seem like they belonged together. She'd been a little jealous of Vanessa since the day they got to London. *Maybe that's all it is,* Stephanie thought. *The fact that Vanessa is so pretty . . . and the fact that Corey seems to like her!*

* * *

Fifteen minutes later Stephanie had nearly finished collecting signatures on the birthday card. Only three people hadn't signed it: Ian, Corey, and Stephanie herself.

"To my dear Stephanie, we'll always have London," Ian said as he opened the card and prepared to write.

Stephanie laughed. "This isn't for *me.* It's for Ms. Donato—for her birthday," she told Ian.

"Oh. Well, I've written in fountain pen, I don't know if I can erase it." He frowned at the card.

"You have not," Stephanie said as she glanced at the card. "Just sign it, okay, Ian?"

"Anything for you," Ian said with a wink. He tapped the pen against his leg, then started to write. "To my dear Ms. Donato. We'll always have London, baby," he said slowly as he signed the card.

"You did not write that!" Stephanie said with a giggle as she took the birthday card from Ian.

"No. Don't be ridiculous. I write romantic notes only to you," Ian said.

Stephanie read what he'd written: "For Ms. Donato, happy birthday from all of England—and me, Ian." "Nice job," she told him as she moved on. She stopped in front of Corey, who was slumped in a chair. He was reading a British film magazine and didn't bother to look up at her.

"Um, Corey? You're the last one. Could you sign this card for Ms. Donato?" Stephanie asked politely.

Corey glanced up at her. His expression was very cool—hostile, almost.

"I'm sorry to interrupt your reading," Stephanie said, a bit surprised by the way Corey was glaring at her. "It'll only take a second."

Corey took the birthday card from her. He scribbled his signature, then handed it back, all without saying a word.

"Thanks," Stephanie said. *Why is he in such a bad mood?* she wondered.

Stephanie quickly studied the card for any handwriting that looked like the note she'd received from "Edwina." None of the signatures looked like the writing on the warning note. So much for her plan to reveal the identity of the fake ghost. But at least Ms. Donato had a really nice birthday card coming her way!

Stephanie was lying on her bed, going over a London guidebook that night, when there was a knock at the bedroom door.

"Allie?" Tiffany pushed open the door. "Remember when we were talking about what we brought? Did you say you had a spare toothbrush with you?"

"Sure, I have an extra new one," Allie said. "My mom insisted on my bringing two of everything—just in case. Do you need it?"

"If you don't mind," Tiffany said. "I think I threw mine out by mistake, but I'm not sure. I can't find it *anywhere.*"

"Hold on and I'll get it for you," Allie said. She pulled her suitcase out of the closet.

"Are you getting ready for bed already?" Stephanie asked as she rubbed her eyes.

"Well, it is almost eleven," Tiffany said.

"Whoa. I didn't realize that!" Stephanie sat up and swung her legs over the edge of the bed. "I was going to take a shower tonight, so I wouldn't have to take the time in the morning."

"You're getting so efficient at this traveling thing, it's almost *scary,*" Darcy teased her. "Next thing you know, you'll have all wrinkle-free clothes." She held up a wadded ball of T-shirts that was lying on top of her dresser. "Which is more than I can say for me."

"We have an iron in our room," Tiffany offered.

"Thanks," Darcy said. "Maybe I'll borrow it later."

Stephanie opened the top drawer of her

dresser to take out her nightshirt. She always folded it and left it in the same place. But when she pulled it out, she couldn't believe her eyes.

Her nightshirt had been cut, and there was a note for her on top of it!

"Steph?" Darcy asked. "What is it?"

"It's not moths, is it?" Tiffany asked. "I hate moths. Of course, I hate the smell of mothballs even more, so I don't know which is worse—"

Allie came up beside Stephanie and gasped. "Oh, my gosh. Look at this!" She grabbed the nightshirt and held it up. The hole cut into it was the shape of a heart. In place of the cotton material, a black paper heart had been loosely stitched to the shirt.

"Oh, well. Looks like I'm sleeping in a T-shirt and shorts from now on," Stephanie joked.

"This isn't funny! Someone's really out to get you," Allie said. "First the dried rose, now this—"

"What does the note say this time?" Darcy wanted to know.

"*This* time?" Tiffany turned white as a sheet.

"'S.T.,'" Stephanie read out loud. "'Your heart is in danger, and so are you. Beware. Edwina.'"

"I knew it!" Tiffany cried. "I knew that when Ian sang that song to you today, it would bring on another visit from Edwina. She just can't stand to see someone else have a boyfriend."

Stephanie laughed. "You mean to tell me that an English ghost from the 1800s was hanging out in Covent Garden today? Watching *karaoke?*"

"Well, she's a ghost, she can go anywhere. Obviously," Tiffany responded.

"Right," Stephanie said as she rolled her eyes. This was getting completely out of control! There was no ghost leaving notes, a dead flower, and a torn nightshirt for her. It was someone real—someone she knew. Which meant the so-called ghost was staying in Kent House, just down the hall. . . .

Whoever it was owed Stephanie a new nightshirt—and a big explanation!

CHAPTER 8

“Now, is everyone ready to view our footage so far?” Mr. Blith asked the next morning. “Places, people. Ready and . . . action!”

Just before he pressed Play, Vanessa rushed into the editing room. Stephanie couldn’t help noticing that she looked a bit like Rene’s twin. Vanessa wore a short pink dress with chunky black wedge sandals and a large pink barrette in her hair. She definitely had the Flamingo style down cold.

“So sorry I’m late,” she said as she took a seat by the door. “I had to call my mum, and she went on and on about this party they’re having tonight— Anyway, sorry.”

"Not a problem," Mr. Blith said.

Stephanie noticed Vanessa glance over at Corey and wave hello. Corey briefly waved back. He looked as if he were admiring Vanessa for a second. Then quickly he turned his attention to the monitor at the front of the room again.

"And here we go . . . take two!" Mr. Blith said.

Stephanie leaned forward in her chair to catch a clear view. Soon everyone was laughing—whether at people singing karaoke, or Ian and Sean's joking around in the Café-in-the-Crypt. There was even a shot of a juggler in Covent Garden dropping plastic balls on Ms. Donato's head.

"Very nice work," Mr. Blith said when they finished the first few sections of tape.

"I don't remember anyone taking those shots at St. Martin-in-the-Fields," Sean said.

"I was being sneaky," Darcy said. "Remember how many pillars there were to hide behind? We were filming before you guys even knew where we were."

Stephanie smiled uneasily as she remembered Ian kissing her that day. They'd *thought* they were alone!

Next they watched the film that Stephanie had shot when she was at the Doc Martens store. Everyone laughed as Mr. Blith fast-forwarded the tape of Darcy racing around to check out every pair of shoes in the place.

"Call *The Guinness Book of World Records!* You ought to win the shopping category," Ian joked. He turned to look at Stephanie. "Brilliant work, luv. I especially like the ceiling shots of the flashing lights."

Stephanie laughed. "Are you serious?"

"Dead serious," Ian said. "Catches the atmosphere in that place."

Stephanie waited for Corey to say that her footage was awful, that it lacked depth or concentration. Anything! But either he thought it was fine—or he wasn't paying very close attention, because he was too busy staring at Vanessa.

I can't believe that I actually miss our fights, Stephanie thought. *What's wrong with me?*

"So, um, Corey. What did you think?" Stephanie asked when Mr. Blith ejected the first tape and prepared to insert another.

Corey shrugged as he tied the laces on his shoes. "Pretty decent work. I don't see anything wrong with it," he said.

"Well . . . any suggestions?" Stephanie asked.

"Nope." Corey leaned over to pick up a scrap of paper on the floor.

Stephanie couldn't help feeling stung. In the

past, he'd have jumped all over her and told her a million things she was doing incorrectly. It might have been annoying, but at least she knew that he cared. What was wrong with him? Why was he being so cold to her?

"I'm so glad we get to sit together today." Ian squeezed Stephanie's hand as they slid onto a bench later that afternoon.

The entire group had tickets to see *Romeo and Juliet* at the reconstructed Globe Theatre. The theater had been built to replicate the original theater where William Shakespeare's plays had been performed.

Stephanie was completely in awe. "I've never been anyplace like this before," she told Ian as she gazed around. "It's amazing!"

The stage of the outdoor theater had a thatched roof, and wooden bench seats curved all around the stage.

"It's all right," Ian said with a shrug. "I've been here a hundred times, so it's nothing special."

"What?" Stephanie asked. "But it hasn't been open that long. How can you—"

Ian grinned. "Just kidding. I've never been here, either. And the play hasn't even started yet, but I'm already sold."

"It's sort of like time travel, isn't it?" Darcy asked as she sat next to Sean at the end of their row.

"Shh! It's starting," Ms. Blith said.

"But we're supposed to film—"

"Not now," Ms. Blith said. "After the show!"

Stephanie couldn't believe she was about to see *Romeo and Juliet*—in London. Could this trip get any better?

"So, Ms. Tanner, what did you think of the play?" Ian asked after the actors and actresses had taken their final bows and left the stage.

Stephanie looked at him and saw that he was filming her. She stood up and brushed the tears off her cheeks. She was a little embarrassed at being caught nearly sobbing—but then she noticed that Allie and Darcy were crying, too.

"It was incredible!" she said breathlessly.

"Incredible? Well, that's high praise," Ian said. "Do you mind elaborating on that a little?"

"Um, I don't know what to say." Stephanie rolled her program over and over in her hands. "What do you want to know? It was the best play ever."

"What was so good about it?" Ian asked.

Stephanie cried into a tissue, then blew her nose.

"That good, huh?" Ian nodded. "High praise indeed."

"Stop it!" Stephanie said, laughing.

"Would you say you give it . . . well, let's say . . . four tissues? Or five?" Ian asked.

"The acting was amazing. Romeo was completely convincing," Stephanie said through her sniffles. "And Juliet, too. And she . . . and he . . . they . . . well, it was just so tragic. I'd always heard about the play, but now that I've seen it, I just can't even put into words how . . ."

"Incredible it is?" Ian suggested.

Stephanie nodded. "Exactly."

"Well, there you have it, ladies and gentlemen," Ian said. "Theater critic Stephanie Tanner has pronounced the play an *incredible* smash hit." He turned off the camera and slung his arm around Stephanie's shoulders. "And she's never wrong. About anything."

"Right," Stephanie said. "Now, do you have any more tissues or what?"

After dinner that night, everyone gathered to watch Ian's video of post-play interviews. Unfortunately, though he had talked with a few people during intermission, his longest interview was with Stephanie. Stephanie cringed as she saw her tear-streaked face on the monitor.

She felt so embarrassed when everyone saw her crying, she felt like running out of the room! *But at least my reaction was authentic,* she told herself. *I can't help it if the play was sad!*

"Just a minute—I think I hear Ms. Donato coming in," Mr. Blith said as he jumped up. "We've got to get the candles lit on her birthday cake! Just pause the tape—I'll be right back. And get ready to sing."

As soon as Mr. Blith was gone, Rene stood up and perched on the windowsill. "It's a shame we can't use any of that video. I mean, it's hopeless," Rene declared.

"Why is that?" Ian asked.

"Because Stephanie's so muddled and nothing she says makes any sense," Rene said. "She just goes on and on without saying anything of any value—"

"That's not true," Ian interrupted.

"Well. I can see why you're defending her, because you did the interview," Rene said spitefully. "But I still say we couldn't even make it look good in the editing bay."

Stephanie had heard more than enough. Rene couldn't just sit there and cut her down in front of the entire class! "Well, maybe you couldn't. Because you don't know the first thing about editing," Stephanie shot back.

"Neither do you!" Rene replied. "We all know that Corey did the final edit in Paris—the one you tried to take credit for."

"That's not true!" Corey interjected. "Stephanie did plenty of the work."

Stephanie looked over at Corey. "Thank you."

"Well, I still don't believe it," Rene said. "Why don't you prove it to us and actually edit something this time around?"

"Fine." Stephanie glared right back at her. "I will!"

Mr. Hanley walked into the viewing room. "You will what?" he asked Stephanie. "Sing 'Happy Birthday,' I hope? Ms. Donato's on her way, and Mr. and Ms. Blith are right behind her with the cake."

"Stephanie just said she'll edit her team's next shoot," Rene declared.

"Oh? Is that so?" Mr. Hanley nodded to Stephanie. "Sounds good to me."

Stephanie smiled uneasily. Did she really want that much responsibility? But it was too late to back out now.

As Ms. Donato walked into the classroom, and

everyone shouted out "Happy Birthday!" Allie leaned over to whisper in Stephanie's ear.

"I don't know about the Edwina stuff, but Rene is plotting something with the video," Allie said. "I wish I could figure out what it is!"

Great, Stephanie thought. First an imaginary ghost was threatening her—now Rene. *Just what I need!*

CHAPTER 9

"Welcome to Dressed by Dex!" Vanessa opened the door to a shop on Carnaby Street. "This is the number one place right now for bands to shop."

"And for all of us who want to *look* like we're in bands," Ian added.

"I can see why," Stephanie said as she followed Vanessa into the clothing store. There were racks of wildly colored leather jackets, leopard print tights, torn and ripped jeans, and silver and gold lamé tops. Photos of bands, along with giant concert posters, covered the walls. The back wall was covered with platform shoes and boots. There was even a giant cubby filled with dozens of pairs of loud striped socks and tights. Lava lamps and hanging bead curtains decorated the place. The smell of incense filled the air.

Darcy gazed around the store, her eyes wide as she took in everything. "Steph, have you ever seen so much leather? And in such bizarre colors?" she asked. "Too bad I already spent my extra money on those new Docs—I could go wild here."

"And you'd look wild, too," Stephanie said. She took one of the boots off the wall and slipped it on. "The heel on this is about six inches!" she told Darcy with a laugh as she balanced herself against a rack of belts. "I can barely walk—look, I'm staggering. How can anyone perform onstage in these?"

"Lots and lots of practice," Ian said as he pulled a tall, shockingly pink top hat made of fake fur onto his head. "What do you say, girls? Am I ready for MTV?"

"Not exactly," Vanessa told him with a frown. "But I thought we could have a fashion show. You guys try stuff on and I'll film you coming out of the dressing room," Vanessa said.

"I think I'll try on this." Ian held up a large collar studded with rhinestones. "Is this for rock stars? Or for rock stars' pets? I can't tell."

Stephanie giggled as she picked up a dress

made of bamboo. The small tan pieces of wood rattled against one another and made a very pretty sound. "I'll try this on, then," she said. "*Over* my clothes."

She and Darcy picked out a couple of different outfits to try on and each chose a booth. Sean and Ian grabbed vinyl jumpsuits, and Tiffany took a couple of different dresses into the dressing room with her. Stephanie saw Corey pick out a T-shirt with a dozen different logos plastered on it, and shiny black pants made of thick nylon.

Clare was helping with the lighting, and Vanessa set the camera on a tripod to film while Mr. Blith spoke with the store manager to get permission to shoot there. Stephanie couldn't believe how organized they were getting at making their documentary. It was going like clockwork lately.

She breezed out of the dressing room wearing a furry black T-shirt over striped flare pants.

"Outrageous, baby!" Ian cried as he gave her a thumbs-up.

Stephanie cracked up laughing when she saw what Ian and Sean had on—identical white sequined jumpsuits. "You look like those old pictures of Elvis Presley!"

"Come on, Stephanie—model for us!" Vanessa instructed.

Stephanie twirled around on her heels in front of the camera. A few seconds later Darcy danced out of the dressing room in a tight black miniskirt, thigh-high suede boots, and a tank top. Behind the girls, Sean and Ian posed with a belt rack as a microphone.

Then Tiffany strolled out of the dressing room to join the group. She was wearing a dress patterned after the flag of Great Britain that wrapped around her like a beach towel.

"Come on, Tiffany—dance with us!" Sean said.

Stephanie laughed as Tiffany tried to take a few dance steps in her platform sandals. She lost her balance, stumbled, and crashed into a guy wearing a baseball cap.

"Oh, my gosh, I'm *so* sorry!" Tiffany apologized as she took a step back.

The guy's baseball cap was knocked off his head.

Stephanie stared at his face. "It can't be," she said under her breath.

Vanessa abandoned the camera so quickly, she nearly knocked it onto the floor. "Excuse me, aren't you Ciaran, from the Boggarts?" she asked politely.

"Is it really *him?*" Darcy asked in a whisper.

"No *way!*" Tiffany shrieked.

"Shh," the boy said as he put a finger to his lips. "Please, keep it quiet. The rest of my mates are just coming in, and if anyone on the street knows we're in here—"

Stephanie glanced out the front window of the shop. She saw three boys climbing out of an old pale-orange station wagon. They were wearing hats and glasses so they wouldn't be recognized. But Stephanie could tell that it was the rest of the band—Patrick, the drummer who looked like Ian, and the two guitarists, Dugan and A.L. Stephanie couldn't believe it. They were even cuter in person than they were in their videos—if that was possible!

But why are they driving around in a beat-up old car? she wondered. Their CD had been on the top of the charts for the last four months. *Couldn't they afford the biggest limo in the world?*

"So, ah, what band are you all in?" Ciaran asked.

"We're the Nobodies," Ian joked. "You probably haven't heard of us."

Ciaran laughed as his friends came up behind him. "Well, not yet . . ."

"What's going on?" A.L. asked. "Who are these . . . strangely dressed new friends of yours?" He surveyed Ian and Sean and shook his head.

"We're fans. And we're so excited to see you!" Cynthia said. "We love your music—all of us do."

"And we have a huge favor to ask you," Vanessa said. "First of all, I've got to be your biggest fan. You have no idea how much stuff of yours I've collected! But I want to ask if I can have one more thing for my collection."

"Hm." Ciaran studied the cap he'd just picked up. "Well, this isn't very exciting, but I suppose you could have this."

"Actually, I was thinking more along the lines of *this.*" Vanessa pointed to the camera. "Could we put you in our documentary video? We're filming a tour of the hottest spots for teens in London. And since you're here, and we're here . . . it would be an awesome combination." She smiled at Ciaran.

His green eyes sparkled as he smiled back at her. "Sounds great. Where do we start?"

"First off, I have a question." Tiffany stepped forward.

"Hold on—let me get the camera started." Vanessa raced back behind the tripod. "I don't want to miss a thing!"

"I have an idea. How about if we each ask a question of one of them?" Stephanie suggested.

"I love that idea—it'll be really funny on tape,

considering how we're dressed," Corey said.

"Okay, if you're ready . . . Wait a second." Vanessa stopped taping. "Would you guys like to change your clothes first? Comb your hair? Anything?"

"Of course not," Dugan said. "This is a documentary, right? You catch life as it is."

"Life, in this case, being dirty, greasy hair." Patrick lifted his hat off his head. "Looks like maybe I should try on one of those wigs over there." He headed across the store, and Clare followed him.

"Okay, me first!" Tiffany said as she positioned herself in front of the camera. "All right. A.L., here's the question I've been *dying* to ask." She cleared her throat. "Your name. It's so mysterious. What does A.L. stand for?"

Stephanie turned to Darcy and rolled her eyes. "Everyone knows *that,*" she whispered.

A.L. laughed. "I'm sorry, I thought you were going for something really in-depth there. A.L.? It's for Angus Leif. I thought that was on all the CD notes. Wasn't it?"

Tiffany's face turned pink. "Oh. Well then, I have another question." She adjusted the British-flag dress that was wrapped tightly around her. "Um . . . what's your favorite song?"

"Rats, I was going to ask that," Darcy said. "Now what am I going to ask?"

"Ask Ciaran if he wants to go out on a date," Stephanie whispered. "In that outfit, how could he turn you down?"

Darcy giggled as she tugged at the miniskirt's hem. "Shut up!"

"Anyway, never mind you—what am *I* going to ask?" Stephanie wondered.

Ian leaned over Stephanie's shoulder and whispered, "Ask him if Patrick is my long-lost twin brother!"

Stephanie grinned as Ian's breath tickled her ear. He and Patrick really did look an awful lot alike. They were both completely adorable. But nobody could be as cute as Ciaran when he sang, she thought. They were so lucky to get the band in their documentary!

She bit her lip as she stepped up to the microphone and found herself face-to-face with Ciaran. "My question is, how did you get started in music? How did you know you wanted to be a singer, and did you have voice training, and—"

"Hold on." Ciaran laughed. "I thought it was one question per person." He winked at Stephanie.

She laughed, embarrassed. "Sorry."

"No problem. Just wanted to give you a hard time," Ciaran teased. "Now, to my answers . . ."

Later that afternoon Stephanie sat at a desk in front of the monitor to screen their Boggarts' video. *Maybe I should thank Rene for forcing me to edit today's tape,* she thought. She couldn't wait to see all the footage they had of the Boggarts. *I probably won't cut anything at all!*

Vanessa and Corey had gone for a walk, but they had told Stephanie they'd come upstairs to help her as soon as they got back.

A walk sounded very romantic to Stephanie. She found it a little hard to believe that Corey could be *that* romantic. *I guess he and Vanessa made a real connection. And I should be happy for him. But it still bothers me,* Stephanie thought.

"Knock, knock." Ian poked his head in through the open doorway. "Can I help?"

"Hey, Ian. No thanks," Stephanie said. "You can watch if you want, though."

"I think I'll work on something on-line, actually," Ian said as he sat down in front of the computer.

Stephanie started to concentrate on the editing work. She played the video back on the monitor. Using the mouse, she could select which images to paste and rearrange. But she had hardly done anything, when suddenly the screen went completely blank.

What's going on? she wondered. She turned the Power button on the monitor off and then back on. Nothing happened. She pressed Rewind to start over. Then she hit Play. There was a whirring sound, and then the player shut off—completely!

Stephanie tried to eject the tape. But it wouldn't come out of the machine! She pulled on it until the cartridge came out. When she finally had it in her hands, half of the tape was stuck in the machine—the other half was spilled out onto her lap, and draped along the floor!

No! This can't be happening! Stephanie thought as Corey and Vanessa walked into the editing room.

"Can we see what you've edited so far?" Vanessa asked. Then her eyes landed on the crumpled, mangled videotape. "What's that? What have you done?"

"I don't know, I didn't mean to . . ." Stephanie stammered.

Corey stared at the strings of tape. "How could you have done that?"

"I don't know!" Stephanie said. "I had just started to edit it—and I was cutting something to paste, and then the screen went blank, and—"

"You destroyed the videotape," Corey said.

"That's the best thing I've ever *done,* Stephanie. Television crews would kill to get that kind of footage with the Boggarts—and I got it! But you—you ruined it!" Vanessa yelled.

"I'm sorry," Stephanie said. "I'm so sorry!" She was starting to feel like a CD with an annoying skip. But she couldn't say *sorry* enough!

Vanessa stormed out of the classroom. Corey followed her.

"That's some bad luck," Ian said softly when they were gone. "But don't worry about it, Stephanie."

"How can I not worry about it?" Stephanie clutched her hands. "I trashed the best video we've gotten so far."

"Hey, look at it this way. Their music videos are on TV, so who needs one more? I'm sure the world can go on without hearing about Ciaran's new leather pants."

But Ian's jokes weren't what Stephanie wanted to hear right then. Nothing could make up for what she'd done!

CHAPTER 10

◆ ◀ ✦ ◆

Stephanie curled up in a chair in the Kent House library after dinner. Everyone else was watching a movie upstairs, but Stephanie didn't feel like joining the group.

They're probably laughing and having a great time. Except Vanessa. She wouldn't even look at me at dinner!

Stephanie knew that Vanessa wouldn't want her to be enjoying the movie with everyone else. Not after the way Stephanie had botched the perfect video of the Boggarts that afternoon. Vanessa was never going to forgive her—Stephanie couldn't even forgive herself! She felt so terrible, she wished she had never come on the trip. She didn't know how to edit—Rene was right. She shouldn't be allowed to help with the London documentary anymore because she'd only ruin the rest of it!

She clutched a pillow to her chest and gazed out at the garden. At night, small paper lanterns stretched along the hedges to light the walkway. As Stephanie stared at them, her eyes blurred with tears.

There was a knock on the heavy wooden door to the library. Stephanie turned toward it and brushed at her eyes with her sweatshirt sleeve.

"*Here* you are," Darcy said as she walked into the library.

"We've been looking all over for you," Corey said.

Stephanie sat up in the chair. She was surprised that Corey was looking for her with Darcy—instead of Ian. Wasn't Corey as furious with her as Vanessa was? Shouldn't he be upstairs with Vanessa? "I thought you guys were watching the movie," Stephanie said.

"We were, but I got worried when I didn't see you," Darcy said. "I knew you were probably sitting here, feeling terrible."

Stephanie nodded as she stuffed the pillow behind her back.

"But you shouldn't be," Darcy said. "It was a mistake. We know you didn't mean to erase the tape. And we forgive you."

"Vanessa's never going to forgive me," Stephanie said glumly. She looked up at Corey. "Is she? I mean, do *you* forgive me?" Stephanie knew that Corey's opinion was ultimately more important to her than Vanessa's. She'd known him longer, and would be spending a few more weeks filming with him. Not to mention going to school with him when they got back home!

"Of course I do," Corey said. "And I'm sorry I sounded so angry earlier. I'm just upset about what happened! But I know it's not your fault."

"I'm upset, too," Stephanie said. "Because I swear I didn't do anything wrong. I *swear.* But it doesn't matter, because now it's like the tape never existed."

Corey sighed and sat down across from her. "Look, you're right. The situation is bad. It's very bad."

Stephanie tossed the pillow at him. "I thought you were looking for me to make me feel better, not worse."

"Hey, I said it was bad, but it's not the end of the world!" Corey told her.

"It is to Vanessa," Stephanie said. "I have to find a way to make it up to her."

"I don't see how you can," Corey said.

"Too bad we can't start today over," Darcy said. "Just click our heels and it would be morning all over again. We'd go to Dressed by Dex, we'd bump into the Boggarts again and film them, and—"

Darcy's on to something, Stephanie thought. "That's it!" she said as she sat up in the leather chair.

"What? You're going to turn back time?" Corey joked.

"No, but I can find the Boggarts again, and film them," Stephanie said. "That's the only way to make it up to Vanessa."

"But she's their number one fan," Darcy said. "If she doesn't know where they are, how are *you* going to find them?"

"Hey, they were in London today, they'll be in London tomorrow," Stephanie said, determined. "How hard can it be to track down the world's most popular boy band?"

"Have you *looked* at a map of London lately?" Corey asked. "This city is huge. Stephanie, that's crazy. You can't do it."

"You just said the magic word, Corey. Don't

ever tell Stephanie she *can't* do something. Because she'll find a way." Darcy took Stephanie's hand and pulled her up from the cushioned chair. "Come on, Steph. Let's go upstairs to the computer and start checking the Internet for the Boggarts!"

The next morning Stephanie crept downstairs before the sun rose. No one else was awake. She glanced at the grandfather clock in the front hallway. It wasn't even five o'clock yet!

It was too bad that Ms. Blith had come by the night before and ordered Stephanie to get off-line and go to bed. She had wanted to stay up all night searching fan club sites, until she found out where they were. But so far she had turned up nothing. Now she had even less time to find the Boggarts.

But maybe there's still a chance, she thought as she grabbed the morning newspapers from the entry table. She raced into the drawing room and sat on the floor to look at them. She yawned as she flipped through the first paper. It was full of international news and political commentary—but no news of the Boggarts.

Stephanie opened the second paper and gasped. There were the Boggarts, right on the cover! "Boggarts Bop to Shop" was the headline—and the photograph showed the band coming out of Dressed by Dex!

Stephanie's heart sank. *We had that shot,* she thought. *We had better ones—we were there!* She skimmed the article quickly for any information about their upcoming appearances and plans. But the reporter wrote only about the clothes Ciaran and A.L. had purchased. After searching it for more details, Stephanie stuffed that paper under the sofa. If Vanessa saw it, she'd get furious all over again.

Stephanie slumped against the sofa as she opened the third paper. Nothing. It was useless. She might as well admit it. Now she'd have to sit around and wait for everyone else to get up. She reached over to turn on the radio. A Boggarts song was playing. Stephanie sighed. She couldn't escape them! She was about to turn off the radio, when the song ended and the disc jockey came on.

"That was our very own Boggarts. And as we promised you yesterday, if you're awake now and listening—which is a very big if—I've got an extra-special announcement," the disc jockey said. "We're announcing this only once, for reasons that will become clear in a moment. And we're announcing it this early for the same reason. We're trying to prevent total, absolute chaos. So, are you ready?"

Stephanie held her breath as the deejay played a clip of screaming girl fans who were all yelling Ciaran's name. Stephanie sat up. Was this going to be about the Boggarts?

"Yes, you're ready. This fine radio station is sponsoring a signing party. That's right. You, us, the Boggarts, one day only, two hours only, in fact—this morning, nine A.M., Kangaroo Music, King Street, get their latest CD at a specially reduced price, get a signature, but get there, people! And, er, don't tell your friends. Because ten seconds after I say this, there will be a line—I guarantee it!"

Stephanie stared at the radio. "Yes!" she cried as she pumped her fist in the air.

She wanted to wake up Vanessa right then and tell her the good news. But before she did, she wanted to think it through. If they tried to film the Boggarts at a public appearance, they'd never get the kind of close-ups and in-depth conversation they had on the original tape. The CD store would be mobbed.

But if she went on her own, maybe she could get a quick word with the band—and set up an appointment to meet privately.

Stephanie raced to the library to find a street map of London. She found Kent House on the map, then looked for the street where Kangaroo Music was. She wasn't a hundred percent sure, but it looked like she could walk to the store!

The only problem was, how did she get there right away, before the line stretched all the way to Paris? How did she sneak off from the rest of the group?

Stephanie lay on her bed and coughed a few times into a tissue. "I just don't feel well," she told Ms. Blith. The rest of the girls all stood around her bed. It was almost eight o'clock, and Stephanie was hoping the group would leave as planned—at eight-fifteen. That *might* give her enough time to get to the CD store before the Boggarts arrived.

"Can I get you anything?" Allie asked.

"No, it's okay," Stephanie said. She felt bad about lying to Darcy and Allie—but she had to do it.

"You shouldn't have stayed up all night on the computer, Stephanie," Ms. Blith said. "Now you're going to miss seeing the Houses of Parliament, which is a highlight of this trip!"

"It'll be thrilling, I'm sure," Rene commented under her breath.

"Sorry you're sick," Clare said, concerned.

"Yeah, it's really too bad," Vanessa said half-heartedly. She seemed to be glad that Stephanie wouldn't be going with them.

"I'm sorry," Stephanie said again. At least now she could hope that she'd make it up to Vanessa. "I didn't mean to get so overtired and run-down," she told Ms. Blith.

"No, of course you didn't," Ms. Blith said. "Well, I'd better stay home with you. Which means I'll miss the tour, which I really don't want to do, but if you're not well—"

"Oh, no—you don't have to stay!" Stephanie said quickly. *Because that will ruin my entire plan!*

"You need a chaperone," Mrs. Donato said. "We can't just leave you here at Kent House by yourself!"

"Especially not with *ghosts* flitting around," Clare said. "I wouldn't stay here by myself for a million pounds."

"But I'm not alone," Stephanie said. "Mrs. Worthington is here. I've already told her that I'm going to be hanging around here this morning. She said she'd stop in and check on me every hour or so." Stephanie smiled at her teachers. It was a flat-out lie, but hopefully no one would ever find out. She had work to do!

"All right, then," Ms. Blith said. "That will work just fine, because we'll be coming back for lunch. So just rest in bed, and take it easy."

"Sure thing," Stephanie said. *If taking it easy includes rushing to Kangaroo Music to see the Boggarts!*

CHAPTER 11

◆ ◀ ✦ ◆

I'm too late.

Stephanie stopped outside Kangaroo Music. She was panting and out of breath. She had run the whole way from Kent House, desperate to make up for lost time. But it didn't matter. The line stretched from the door, down the block, around the corner, and down another block. . . . Stephanie couldn't even see where it ended.

She tried to catch her breath as she stood on the sidewalk across the street and looked at the mob scene. If she could even get in the door—never mind being able to talk to the Boggarts—she'd consider herself lucky. Hundreds of other girls had gotten there before her!

Nevertheless, she decided to wait in line. She had to stay positive, or she wouldn't accomplish anything. *Who knows? Maybe they autograph things really, really quickly.* If all four guys in the band signed the CDs, she thought, she wouldn't stand a chance. But if each customer got only one signature, they could get four customers out of the store at a time.

Stephanie shook her head. She was starting to think like her math teacher back at John Muir, but word problems weren't going to help her now. She was in for the long haul, she realized as she took her place at the end of the huge line.

"We don't stand a chance," the girl in front of her was saying to a friend.

"No, we don't," her friend replied. "But at least we're not dead last anymore. That's something." She turned around to Stephanie. "Sorry."

"It's okay," Stephanie said with a smile. "I know it's totally hopeless, but I'm going to try to get in, anyway."

"Hey, an American! Where are you from?" the girl asked.

Soon Stephanie and the two girls were caught up in a fun conversation. They talked, laughed, exchanged e-mail addresses—Stephanie had a great time.

After a while, Stephanie glanced at her watch and saw that over an hour and a half had gone by. They had moved only about a block, and there were still a hundred girls in front of them. She knew she wasn't going to get in to see the Boggarts. Her plan was falling apart! *What am I going to do?* Stephanie thought as she chewed her thumbnail. She tried to think of ways she had used to meet bands before. But she hadn't exactly done this before!

The only thing I can do is try to catch them on their way out, she realized. *Which means guessing which back door they'll use—and getting there first!*

"Well, I'd better take off," Stephanie told her new friends in line, Joanna and Diana. "I need to meet some people, and it doesn't look like this is going to happen, so . . ."

"It doesn't look good for us, does it?" Joanna frowned.

Diana punched her playfully on the arm. "I *told* your mum to let us skip breakfast—but did she? No. We miss the Boggarts because she insists on raisin scones."

Stephanie laughed. "Oh, well. It was great meeting you both. Good luck, and don't forget to write!"

"Bye, Stephanie!" they both called out.

Stephanie waved as she jogged down the block toward the rear of the store. A crowd had already gathered there, but Stephanie told herself it didn't matter. She had to talk to the Boggarts—somehow.

As she ran, she suddenly spotted an old, beat-up orange station wagon parked on the side street. *That's the same car the Boggarts were riding in when they came to Dressed by Dex yesterday!* Stephanie thought excitedly. Instead of using a limo, they traveled in a used car, to escape the crowds. *I hope no one knows that but me!*

Stephanie crouched beside the car. She glanced at her watch. It was nearly eleven—the band should be coming out any minute now.

Suddenly Stephanie heard loud shrieks. *That's them!* She stood up and watched as several security guards surrounded the Boggarts, who were leaving the store. Girls ran alongside the guards to catch a glimpse of the band. Stephanie knew she had to go for it soon—or lose her chance!

She stood up just as the group approached the car. "Ciaran!" she cried as she waved at him. "Ciaran, do you have a second? Please? Ciaran!" Stephanie yelled.

He looked over at the car and caught her eye.

She watched as he said something to the other guys.

"Hey, you're the girl from Dressed by Dex," Ciaran said.

"Um, one of them," Stephanie said nervously as she scrambled to get closer to him. The security guards were already whisking Patrick, A.L., and Dugan into the backseat of the cramped car. "Remember we're shooting a documentary, and it's really important?"

"Sure, of course I remember," Ciaran said. "Make it fast—we've got to bolt before we get hurt!"

"Our tape got ruined!" Stephanie said. "The footage we got is all gone. Can we please meet you again and shoot more tape? Anywhere, anytime—please?" she begged.

Ciaran climbed into the car and shut the door.

Oh, no! Stephanie thought as the crowd pressed against her back, nearly pushing her into the car, too. *He's leaving!*

Suddenly a hand reached out of the window. Stephanie felt a piece of paper being pressed into her palm. Then one of the guards raced the engine, and the car pulled out into traffic. The Boggarts were gone! Hundreds of girls ran down the side street after the departing car.

Stephanie gulped as she opened the slip of paper. On it was a scribbled street address, and the words "2 P.M. tomorrow." It was signed: Be there! Ciaran, etc.

Stephanie wandered back to Kent House in a daze. She couldn't believe it. She had had a private conversation with Ciaran. Maybe it had lasted only ten seconds, but still. She was carrying a piece of paper that he'd written on—for her. Mission accomplished. No one was going to believe this.

As she walked, Stephanie checked her pocket from time to time to make sure the paper didn't fall out. If she lost that address . . .

She stopped and took her pen out of her tote bag. Then she wrote the address on her arm—and on a page from her notebook.

About fifteen minutes later she walked into Kent House and took her tote bag off her shoulder. She nearly dropped it when she saw Mr. Blith standing in the front hallway.

"Stephanie? I thought you were sick, laid up in bed," Mr. Blith said in an angry tone. "Where are you coming from, and what's going on?"

"Well, I needed some fresh air, and—" Stephanie's voice faltered as she saw Ms. Blith come out of the kitchen behind him.

"Stephanie? I've just had a word with Mrs. Worthington," Ms. Blith said.

"Oh?" Stephanie asked.

"She never talked to you this morning and hasn't seen you all day." Ms. Blith put her hands on her hips. "Where have you *been?*"

CHAPTER 12

Stephanie took a deep breath. There was no getting around this. She'd been caught. "I'm sorry," she told Mr. and Ms. Blith. "I didn't want to lie, but there was something I absolutely had to do. I couldn't think of any other way."

"And what was so important that you had to sneak out?" Mr. Blith asked.

Ms. Blith shook her head. "If your father finds out about this, we'll be in serious trouble, Stephanie. You *and* us. We're responsible for you, remember?"

"And this isn't the first time you've gone out without permission," Mr. Blith pointed out. "It happened in Paris as well, but I shouldn't have to remind you of that."

"I know, I know!" Stephanie said. "And I'm sorry. But I had to make it up to Vanessa. You heard how I ruined our tape last night—the tape of the Boggarts. She was devastated. So I spent all last night and this morning figuring out how I could find them," she explained.

"And did you find them?" Ms. Blith asked excitedly. Then she paused. "Wait a minute. I'm not so sure I like the idea of you sneaking around with a rock band."

Stephanie smiled. "I did find them, but don't worry—it was at a music shop with hundreds and hundreds of other people around. They were signing autographs for their new CD."

"Oh." Ms. Blith nodded. "Very good. So did you get a chance to talk to them?"

"It was completely jammed with fans, but I managed to get a quick conversation with them. And they agreed to let us film them again—that is, if *you* say we can," Stephanie said. "It's tomorrow afternoon, and here's the address." She held out the cherished slip of paper Ciaran had given her.

"We'll run this by Mr. Hanley, but it seems all right to me—so far," Mr. Blith said.

"Okay, but, um, don't lose that piece of paper," Stephanie said. "It's the best souvenir I have yet!"

"I'll guard it with my life," Mr. Blith promised. "Now, if this all works out, and if Vanessa gets the tape of the Boggarts she wants . . . well, I can't be too angry about what you did today. You were genuinely trying to fix things, and this is all in the interest of our video."

"However . . ." Ms. Blith said.

Stephanie suppressed a groan. *Here it comes,* she thought.

"You definitely did do something wrong, although you were trying to do the right thing," Ms. Blith continued. "I'm afraid you'll have to stay home this afternoon instead of going to the matinee with us."

Stephanie had been dying to see the dance show they had tickets for, but she nodded. "That makes sense."

"Now, let's go get the others for lunch and tell them the good news about the Boggarts," Ms. Blith said.

Stephanie started to follow her.

"Stephanie? Wait a second," Mr. Blith said.

Stephanie turned around. "What is it?"

"I've been going over and over this in my mind. And I still don't understand how you could have jammed the machine and erased all that Boggarts footage yesterday," he said. "From what you told me, what you did shouldn't have erased anything. Would you mind explaining what happened again?"

"Sure thing." Stephanie told him the steps she had taken in the editing bay. "As far as I know, that's exactly how we edited film the day before." She shrugged.

"Sure sounds like it," Mr. Blith told her. "Let me have a look at it, but I suspect it's not you. It's the machine. Obviously, we won't use that one again until we find out what's wrong with it. But all I can think is that either it's defective—or somebody tampered with it before you got there. I don't like to think that . . ." Mr. Blith took off his cap and rubbed his head. "There's no one in this group who'd pull a stunt like that, I'm sure."

Stephanie briefly thought of Rene, and how she'd practically ordered Stephanie to edit the tape. But she wouldn't mention her suspicions to Mr. Blith—not until she found out more. *If* there was anything more to the story.

She looked up at him and shrugged. "I don't know. All I know is that everyone was furious with me, and I had to fix it."

"And won't it be just awful to see those

Boggarts again," Mr. Blith said with a smile. "I'm sure you're *dreading* it."

Stephanie grinned. "Oh, yeah. Like you wouldn't believe!"

Everyone started filing past on their way to the dining room.

"Hey, Steph! Feeling better?" Darcy asked with a wink. "Ms. Blith just told us that you tracked down Ciaran. That's so awesome!"

"It's not fair. You got to see the Boggarts instead of a bunch of boring politicians in Parliament," Cynthia added with a frown. "How did you find them?"

"I got up early, and I heard about their appearance on the radio," Stephanie confessed. She looked at Vanessa. "I'm sorry, I wanted to tell you. But I thought it would work better if I could set up another shoot—I mean, in case they said no. But I know you're a more devoted fan than I am, and I really wish you could have seen them and—"

"Don't sweat it, Stephanie. You did a nice thing, and I'm thrilled. Just tell me. What were they wearing?" Vanessa asked. "Anything they bought yesterday?"

Stephanie ignored Rene's dirty look and fell into step beside Vanessa. "I'll tell you everything," she said. "Even what color socks they had on."

"Oh, good grief," Ian said as he walked behind them. "You'd think the sun rose and set based on the blasted Boggarts! Didn't you miss *me* this morning?" He threw his arm around Stephanie's shoulders and gave her a squeeze. "There I was, worried sick about you. I couldn't even make fun of our tour guide, I was so blue. And there you were, hanging out with those Irish blokes again."

"I only saw them for about ten seconds," Stephanie said. "Don't worry." She looked around for Vanessa, but she and Rene had already vanished into the dining room. *I might have patched things up, but she still hasn't forgiven me totally,* Stephanie thought.

That afternoon Stephanie was alone in Kent House again. The sky was dark and threatening, and it looked as if the clouds might open up and rain at any second. So instead of sitting outside in the garden as she had planned, Stephanie found a cozy spot in a corner of the library.

Stephanie had brought a notebook and pen down in her tote bag, because she'd planned to write letters while everyone was out. After a few attempts at first sentences, she realized she really wasn't in the mood. She was too tired to write. So she decided to read.

She sorted through a bookshelf until she found an old leather-bound book on the history of the area. Then she curled up in a large, dark burgundy leather chair, and draped her sweatshirt over her as a blanket.

Stephanie leafed through the book until she found a chapter dealing with the Kent family, and the building of the mansion. She read all about the lineage of the family and its background in England. A family tree showed Edwina's name and the year she had passed away.

Stephanie read for a while longer, then closed her eyes. She was tired from staying up late the night before, and getting up early that morning. She was getting very sleepy. *Well, there's no harm in taking a little nap, is there?* she thought just before she slipped off to sleep.

Stephanie woke up feeling hungry. She decided to go into the kitchen to make herself a snack. She got up and walked through the first floor. As she passed by the hall closet, the door slowly opened.

Stephanie sensed a figure behind her and turned around. It was the ghost of Edwina!

"You are not being careful enough," the ghost said.

"You're not real," Stephanie replied. "And I'm not afraid of you!" She turned away and hurried into the dining room.

The ghost was sitting at the head of the table! "I warned you, didn't I? What happens if you ignore my warnings?"

"Nothing!" Stephanie said bravely. "Go away. You're scaring Clare."

"You would be wise to be scared by me, also," Edwina's ghost said. "I know the truth about love!"

Stephanie ignored her and pushed on into the kitchen. I must be imagining all this because I'm so hungry, *she thought.* All I need is a little snack and I'll be fine.

Stephanie opened the pantry door.

Edwina was waiting for her inside. "You are not being careful. I told you," the ghost said. "You'll lose your heart and much more."

"No, I won't!" Stephanie cried. Rushing to get away from the ghost, she crashed into the swinging kitchen door on her way out. The door kept opening and closing, opening and closing, as if a spirit controlled it. Stephanie couldn't get through—she couldn't escape from Edwina!

"Leave me alone!" Stephanie cried. "Let me go!"

* * *

Stephanie woke up in a panic. The sound of the door banging hadn't gone away—it was real. But it wasn't in the kitchen—it was a shutter on the window beside the fireplace, banging in the wind of the rainstorm.

If the noise was real . . . did that mean Edwina was real? Was she still chasing Stephanie? She sat up and turned from side to side, looking for the ghost. She heard footsteps coming down the hall toward the library and clutched her sweatshirt to her chest. The steps stopped outside the library door. A scream rose in Stephanie's throat.

"Hey there, Stephanie, how are you? How was your afternoon?" Ian asked as he strode into the library.

Stephanie was shaking so much, she couldn't answer him at first. So the ghost wasn't real. But her dream had *felt* real. . . .

"What's the matter, luv? Did I wake you up? Are you cold? You're as white as a sheet, Stephanie." Ian sat on the arm of Stephanie's chair. He leaned over to hug her, and rubbed her arms to warm her up. "If you're not careful, you *will* catch a cold."

"No, I'm—I'm o-okay," Stephanie stammered as Vanessa walked into the library.

When Vanessa saw the two of them sitting so close together, she stopped. "Oh. Well, I felt bad about you not going to the show, Stephanie. But I take it you're having a lovely afternoon now," Vanessa said in a bitter tone.

"Stephanie got spooked by being here all alone—I was just reassuring her everything's okay," Ian said. He sounded very nervous, as if he'd been caught doing something he shouldn't.

"Mm-hm. Well, dinner's ready," Vanessa said. "That's the only reason I came in here, to tell you that." She turned and walked briskly out of the library.

"Is she mad at us or something?" Stephanie asked.

"Don't worry about it," Ian said. "She's just in a bad mood because she had to sit behind a lady with big hair at the show. Couldn't see a thing until Mr. Hanley switched seats with her during the intermission."

Stephanie laughed as she got to her feet. She tossed her notebook and pen into her small tote bag. "So, how was the show?" she asked as she followed Ian through the first floor to the dining room. She looked around carefully. Was Edwina really in the coat closet? Or was she waiting in the dining room?

Don't do this! Stephanie told herself. *Don't let a bad dream make you believe in ghosts! Edwina Kent isn't here.*

But she felt herself shiver as she took her seat at the dining table and pushed her tote bag underneath it.

After dinner the group went to a neighborhood restaurant for dessert. Stephanie ordered ice cream and sat down with Darcy and Allie. Ian and Sean were busy joking around with the waitresses. She watched Vanessa sit with Corey at a table for two, while Rene, Tiffany, and Cynthia shared another table.

"I feel like I haven't seen you guys in weeks instead of just one day," Stephanie said after she swallowed her first bite.

"So here's what you missed," Allie said, and then started to describe the day they had had.

"It was all right, but it's not going to compare to seeing the Boggarts again tomorrow," Darcy concluded. "What are you guys going to wear? Do you think we're going to see their London apartment, or is it a hotel, or a studio—"

"Excuse me." Nigel leaned over from the table next to them, where he was sitting. "Does anyone have a pen? I need to make a list for our group's remaining shoots. We're having a slight disagreement."

"Sure—I've got one." Stephanie reached into her tote bag and pulled out her pen.

"And some paper, too, if you've got it," Nigel said. "I don't think a napkin's going to cut it."

"I have this." Stephanie took out her notebook. As she opened it to tear out a blank page for Nigel, a photograph fluttered out onto the floor.

"What's that?" Allie asked.

"I don't know," Stephanie said. She bent down to pick up the picture. It was a copy of an old print, with brown, slightly faded tones. "There's a person here, and she's lying down and . . ." Stephanie stared at the photo in disbelief. Her hands started to shake so much that she could barely hold on to the photo. "It's—it's Edwina Kent—in her casket!"

CHAPTER 13

◆ ◀ ✦ ◆

On the walk home from the restaurant, Corey and Ian caught up with Stephanie. She was still nervous about finding the print of Edwina Kent in her tote bag, but she was trying not to think about it. *It isn't Edwina Kent,* she told herself. *It's someone in this group—someone who was at the restaurant.* That was why she didn't want to show them how upset the whole thing was making her.

"Stephanie, what's going on?" Corey asked as he fell into step with her on the sidewalk. "Darcy just said you keep getting all these messages from the so-called ghost of Edwina. That print isn't the first thing?"

Stephanie shook her head. "No. First there was the dried black rose on my pillow, then someone cut a hole in my nightshirt—"

"You're being completely haunted," Ian said. "But I don't fall for the Edwina Kent story, no matter what Mrs. Worthington believes. Somebody here is trying to scare you, right?" he asked in a soft voice.

"I think so," Stephanie said. "And at first I was mostly just irritated—I thought it was stupid. Now . . ." She didn't want to tell about her nightmare that afternoon. Or that the casket photo gave her chills whenever she thought about it. But apparently, it was written all over her face, because both Corey and Ian acted very concerned.

"You've gone all shaky just thinking about it," Ian said. "Just like you were when I found you in the library this afternoon."

"Stephanie, I know you. You don't get freaked out and scared over nothing," Corey said. "Someone's got a really sick sense of humor, and we're going to find out who it is."

His comments made Stephanie feel a little better. Slowly, as they walked behind the rest of the group through the city streets, she told Corey and Ian about the "ghost" and her messages. "She keeps warning me not to lose my heart," Stephanie said. "And not to fall in love, because it's dangerous."

"I thought it was Shakespeare who said that," Ian joked. *"Romeo and Juliet,* right?" Then he snapped his fingers. "I know. It's a rabid fan of the Boggarts! She saw you talking with Ciaran and—"

"You know what? You might be on to something." Stephanie remembered Tiffany's saying that Ian's karaoke song to Stephanie had somehow brought on another visit from Edwina. "Not about the Boggarts, but . . . maybe there's someone who really doesn't want me to be happy. So whenever it looks like I am . . . whoever it is has to threaten me or scare me."

Rene Salter's name comes to mind, Stephanie thought. But the plan seemed too diabolical even for Rene.

"Well, let's just say that *is* the case." Corey took a roll of toffee out of his jacket pocket and offered pieces to Stephanie and Ian. "If we want to catch this ghost . . . I guess we need to stage some sort of romantic moment for you. Say, for tomorrow night?"

Ian held up his hand. "I volunteer!"

Stephanie laughed as she and Corey exchanged

awkward glances. "I'm pretty sure you were who he had in mind," Stephanie told Ian.

Corey kept looking at her, his brow furrowed.

Oh. Maybe that wasn't what he wanted? Stephanie thought.

"And we'll have to ask your friends for help," Corey said. "While you and Ian are out somewhere—wherever—they and I can hide around Kent House and see who leaves a spooky message for you. We'll catch whoever it is—in the act."

"Okay. But which friends?" Stephanie asked.

"Limit it to the ones you absolutely know and trust," Corey said. "Like Darcy and Allie and . . . well, is there anyone else?"

"Clare, but she'd be too scared," Stephanie said. "I think I could ask Cynthia, though."

"Okay, then." Ian tossed his toffee wrapper into the trash. "One very romantic evening, coming up." He grinned at Stephanie. "Oh, no. Am I going to have to buy you flowers?"

"Keep it simple," Corey said. "The whole point is to expose the phony ghost, remember?"

"Hey, no one said we couldn't have fun with the plan, right?" Ian joked. "But not too much fun. The ghost might flip out if that happened."

Stephanie smiled uneasily. "We definitely wouldn't want that."

As hard as she tried, she couldn't stop being scared by that photo of the casket—and her dream that afternoon. Tomorrow was going to be a huge day. She just hoped their plan would work—and that the ghost was as real as they thought!

CHAPTER 14

"It's two o'clock." Vanessa tapped her boot against the sidewalk. "Where *are* they?"

"They'll be here," Stephanie said boldly. "They promised." *At least I hope they did!* What if Ciaran had forgotten all about the note he'd scribbled so quickly? But he wouldn't have written down this address for no reason, Stephanie reasoned. They had to be upstairs practicing or recording or *something*.

"Okay, but this area is completely deserted." Tiffany looked around at the large warehouses and empty streets. "Why would they be here?"

"Because nobody would find them here and bother them," Cynthia told her. "And it's awesome because once they come out, no one else is going to come along and interrupt us. Right? We can shoot all the film we want."

As long as they actually come out soon, Stephanie thought. She was glad they'd gone ahead and set up their camera, tripod, and light screen. They were ready to start filming as soon as the Boggarts walked out. She glanced at her watch. Now it was two-oh-five.

"And just because this area is a bit . . . deserted, that doesn't mean it's dangerous," Ms. Donato said. "I'm sure plenty or musicians use these buildings for rehearsal space."

"Besides, even if it were dangerous—you've got me to protect you, Tiff," Ian said.

Corey rolled his eyes. "Give me a break, Thornton."

"What? Are you *doubting* my fighting ability?" Ian started to flex his muscles.

Just then the heavy metal door to the building opened. Stephanie's eyes lit up as Ciaran walked out into the bright afternoon sunlight. He was wearing a black leather jacket over a white T-shirt, and old faded jeans. A.L., Dugan, and Patrick followed him out the door and onto the sidewalk.

"Hey, haven't we seen you someplace before?" Dugan joked.

"In better outfits?" A.L. asked.

"Thank you *so* much for coming," Stephanie told them. "I was the one who messed up and erased our tape of you guys. And it means a lot to us that you'd meet us here to film again."

"No problem," Ciaran said. "These things happen, right?"

"We made a tape once, when we were first starting out—to send to record companies," A.L. said. "Only we didn't know much about making tapes. We ended up sending out Ciaran's home movie of his little sister's birthday party. Completely humiliating."

Everyone laughed.

"Hey, I've got an idea," Dugan said. "Since we were just upstairs rehearsing, and our voices are all warmed up . . . why don't we start off with a song?"

"*Would* you?" Vanessa asked.

"You mean—a capella?" Darcy shifted the microphone so that it was closer to them. "That's so awesome!"

"Do you need any help?" Ian cleared his throat. "Because I've been known to win a karaoke contest now and then."

Ciaran laughed. "No, we don't need any help. Not unless anyone's got a guitar on them," he said. "We'll just have to wing it. Ready, guys? Here's a new one we've been working on."

Stephanie glanced over at Corey and Vanessa as the Boggarts started to hum in harmony. Maybe *this* would make up for her big mistake! But instead of catching Vanessa's eye, Stephanie found herself smiling at Corey, who had turned to look at her. He gave her the thumbs-up signal and smiled. Stephanie couldn't have been happier!

"Well, Stephanie—ready for that sunset walk we talked about?" Ian asked that night at the dinner table.

Stephanie nodded. She knew he was announcing their walk in front of everyone as part of their plan to expose the ghost.

"Where are you two going?" Ms. Donato asked.

"Oh, just through the garden and down to the river. We won't be long," Ian promised. "Twenty minutes. Half an hour at most. Then we'll be back."

Stephanie knew Ian was mentioning the time in order to get the so-called "ghost" to take action in their absence. This way, whoever was responsible would need to do something in the next half hour.

Ian walked over to Stephanie's chair and held out his hand. "Hurry, or we'll miss the sunset. I think they're so romantic, don't you?"

Don't overdo it! Stephanie wanted to say as they passed by Corey's chair. Of course, Ian couldn't do anything halfway. It wasn't his style.

As soon as they were outside, Ian put an arm around Stephanie's shoulders. "Should we walk past the dining room like this?" he asked.

"No!" Stephanie said. "I think you made it really clear that we wanted a romantic walk together."

"Good." Ian fidgeted with his watch as they walked down the sloping lawn toward the river. They strolled back and forth along the bank for several minutes. Stephanie didn't enjoy killing time, but this wasn't so bad—after all, she was in London, with a fun, good-looking boy by her side.

About fifteen minutes into their walk, Ian abruptly stopped and turned to face Stephanie. He took Stephanie's hands in his.

"Stephanie, there's something I have to tell you," he announced.

"What?" Stephanie asked. "What's wrong?"

"Well, I feel really bad that I haven't mentioned this before, as it's rather important. And this is going to sound really awful," he said.

"What is?" Stephanie asked. "Ian, I've never seen you so serious. What's going on?"

"I haven't been totally honest with you. See, Vanessa and I . . . well, we were dating before you got here. I mean, we'd been together as a couple for the past six months or so."

"What?" Stephanie was completely shocked. "You have?"

Ian nodded. "Yes. But two weeks ago we got into a huge argument and we broke up."

"Oh." Stephanie didn't know what to say. Was that why Vanessa didn't seem to like her—because she was jealous? "What, um, happened?" she asked.

"She said I was all wrong for her, and she immediately started seeing this other bloke," Ian continued. "It was really awkward, but neither one of us wanted to give up this experience. So, I decided I was going to show her. I decided I was going to go out with the first pretty girl I saw." He looked into Stephanie's eyes. "Which happened to be you."

"You mean, you went out with me only to make Vanessa jealous?" Stephanie couldn't believe it. She'd thought Ian was really interested in her.

"It started out that way, sure," Ian said. "But then I got to know you. And I really like you,

Stephanie." He sighed. "The problem is, I'm also still crazy about Vanessa."

Stephanie sat on a stone bench near the river. She felt like she needed a few minutes to absorb everything Ian had said.

At first she had thought she was definitely falling for Ian. But she also knew that she'd been really jealous of Vanessa whenever she saw her with Corey. She had to admit that when she thought about Ian now, it was more as a friend than a boyfriend—no matter how many sweet things he said to her, or how many times he sang to her. It wasn't the same as her intense connection with Corey. Ian might entertain her, but Corey intrigued her.

Ian sat down beside her. "Do you hate me? Do you wish you'd never come to London? Do you wish you'd never even heard the name Ian Thornton?"

"What? No, of course not," Stephanie said with a laugh.

All of a sudden, she heard footsteps racing toward them. Corey dashed up, smiling and out of breath. "We got it!" he yelled. "We got the ghost!"

"Yes!" Stephanie jumped up and gave him a high five.

Ian leapt to his feet. "So, who is it?"

"You won't believe this. But it's Vanessa," Corey said. "Darcy caught her leaving a message for you, from Edwina. And before *that,* Allie saw her writing the note in the library! She was copying old handwriting from a book."

"Wait a second. So does that mean Vanessa was so jealous of Stephanie being with me . . . that she turned into a ghost?" Ian asked. "Just to get you to stay away from me?"

Corey nodded. "That's what she said. I guess the way you broke up with her really hurt her—"

"*She* broke up with *me,* not the other way around," Ian protested.

"Hold on. I thought Vanessa liked *you,*" Stephanie said to Corey. "You've spent all that time together—and she kissed you."

"I think she tried to like me," Corey said. "And for a while I thought I had a crush on her. But this morning we had a talk and we agreed—we're just friends. Anyway, that's not all."

Ian put his hands on his hips. "You can't tell me someone else was involved in this! It's already ridiculous enough that we dragged you two into it."

"This isn't about me and Stephanie," Corey said. His face turned red. "I mean, not that there is a me and Stephanie," he mumbled. "Anyway—it's what happened in the editing bay. Rene and Tiffany were watching the Boggarts' tape tonight, after Sean and Vanessa edited it on the new machine. Rene told Tiffany that she tampered with the other machine—I'm not sure what she did exactly. But that's why the tape got caught and you erased all the original footage!"

"What? She tampered with the machine? Who heard her say this?" Stephanie asked.

"Cynthia and Ms. Donato were walking into the room to watch the tape, too," Corey explained. "They heard the whole thing. Ms. Donato is talking with Rene right now."

"I'd like to have a talk with her, too!" Stephanie said. "She nearly ruined one of the most fun days on our trip."

"As for me, I think I'd better go have a chat with Vanessa," Ian said. "This is all getting a bit on the ridiculous side. See you guys later!" He jogged back up the garden path.

"I hope Rene gets kicked off this trip," Stephanie said as she turned to follow Ian back to the house. "Can you believe she ruined our video—just to get me in trouble *again?*"

Corey put a hand on Stephanie's arm to keep her from leaving. "I know you probably want to go punch her," he said. "Which is probably not a good idea. And besides . . ." He looked into Stephanie's eyes. "I think you and I need to talk instead."

"You do?" Stephanie asked. Her heart started to beat faster. "Um, about what?"

"About the fact that I could never really have a crush on Vanessa," Corey said. "Because *you're* the one I really like, Stephanie."

CHAPTER 15

Stephanie sat back down on the stone bench. She felt completely overwhelmed. Had Corey just said that he had feelings for her—that he liked her as more than a friend? Did he feel that they were the ones who should be a couple?

"Okay," she said slowly, "let's talk." She looked up at Corey. "I like you, too. But I don't understand something. You've been acting really weird lately, and half the time I don't know if you like me—or you hate me."

Corey sat down beside her. "I know. I'm sorry. It's because I couldn't stand seeing you with Ian. It was driving me crazy when I thought you liked him. Hold on—*do* you like him?"

Stephanie shook her head. "As a friend, yes—but I'm not interested in him. I forgot—you weren't here for *that* conversation. Do you know that Ian paid me so much attention only to make Vanessa jealous?"

"I didn't at the time," Corey said. "I thought you guys really hit it off. I was kicking myself for not telling you earlier that I liked you—back in Paris."

"What?" Stephanie couldn't believe her ears. "You wanted to go out with me then? But you—and Rene—all you did at first was try to help Rene get me in trouble!"

Corey shook his head and laughed. "No. It might have looked like that's what I was doing, because I was too *embarrassed* to tell you the truth."

Stephanie turned to face him. "And what was the truth?"

"I couldn't stand Tristan, and I couldn't stand that you liked him!" Corey admitted. "I helped Rene keep you guys apart only because I didn't want you and Tristan together—*not* because I agreed with anything Rene was actually doing."

Stephanie giggled. "You were helping Rene just so I wouldn't date Tristan? But didn't you know that he had a girlfriend the whole time?"

"No. But I knew he was totally the wrong guy for you," Corey said. He sounded as definite about that as he did about the right way to make a movie.

"So, um . . ." Stephanie kicked at a pebble on the ground. "Who's the right guy for me, then?"

"Who else?" Corey said as he scooted closer to her. "Me. Couldn't you tell the first time we met?"

"You mean when you wouldn't even lend me your *pen* to fill out a luggage tag at the airport?" Stephanie asked. "Or when you yelled at me for dropping your camera? Which I didn't even come close to dropping? Or when you told me everything I did was wrong—"

"Shh," Corey said as he lifted Stephanie's hair off her neck. Then he traced her cheek with his fingers.

Stephanie lifted her lips to his as he pulled her toward him. *Who would have believed this?* she thought as she kissed Corey. *I don't even believe it. Corey Griffin and I are kissing!*

"I'm sorry again about trying to scare you," Vanessa told Stephanie a few days later as they stood outside on the wide steps of Kent House. "It was really idiotic of me. The only thing I can say is that I really must be in love. That, or I'm crazy. Or both." She laughed.

"I forgive you," Stephanie said. "It wasn't fun, but I understand that sometimes we all do strange things."

She glanced around the steps to see if everyone else in her group was outside yet. They were heading off for the third leg of their trip, which would take them to Tuscany, Italy.

"Well, if I ever see the Boggarts again, I'll definitely mention your name," Vanessa said. "I'll tell them to call you when they're ready to shoot their next music video."

"Actually, have them call Corey," Stephanie said. "I still don't trust myself when it comes to making movies."

"You mean you don't trust *Rene,*" Corey whispered in her ear.

"You're right—but I was being serious," she said. "I'd much rather have you edit our next documentary than me."

"You're just being lazy," Corey teased her.

Stephanie grinned. "Sure I am! I want to hang out in the Italian countryside, not work."

"You guys have been fantastic," Ian said as he walked up beside Vanessa. "And very, very understanding. Next time you visit, we promise we won't drag you into our soap opera."

"Oh, I don't know." Stephanie looked over at Corey. "I think it worked out kind of well, actually."

Vanessa smiled. "Well, I'm still really sorry. And about Rene sabotaging that machine—if I'd known she was the kind of person who'd sabotage *our* tape just to get at *you*—I'd never have spent a minute trying to be her friend."

"Are you saying you won't be wearing any more pink clothes anytime soon?" Darcy asked.

"If ever." Vanessa glared at Rene, who was standing with Mr. and Ms. Blith. "At least she's getting another lecture—I hope she gets a hundred more!"

Just then Mr. Hanley pulled up in a blue van. He was going to drop off Stephanie's group at the railroad station. He hopped out of the van and jogged up to the top step. "Everyone? I just heard something on the radio that might interest you." He adjusted his crooked bow tie.

"The Boggarts are doing a concert here?" Tiffany shrieked with excitement. "Then we can't leave—we have to stay!"

"I'm afraid it's not that exciting," Mr. Hanley said. "It's news of a more serious nature." He cleared his throat. "Since you're heading to Italy today, I thought you should know—there's a ring of thieves operating in Tuscany. Supposedly, they're robbing tourists right and left. You've got to be extremely careful—all of you."

"Did they say where in Tuscany?" Ms. Donato asked.

"They did, but I'm drawing a blank right now. I can't remember what town they said." Mr. Hanley frowned.

"Well, we should be okay as long as it's not Siena," Mr. Blith said.

Mr. Hanley snapped his fingers. "That's the town! Siena!"

"Well, then. Hold on to your wallets," Ian joked. "And don't forget what I said about closing those backpack pockets!"

Stephanie squeezed Corey's hand tightly. She knew Italy was going to be fun. But it might be even more exciting than she thought.

What were they getting themselves into?

Don't miss out on any of Stephanie and Michelle's exciting adventures!

FULL HOUSE™ Sisters

When sisters get together... expect the unexpected!

Published by Pocket Books

2012-05

FULL HOUSE™ Michelle

#10: MY BEST FRIEND IS A MOVIE STAR!
(Super Edition)
#11: THE BIG TURKEY ESCAPE
#12: THE SUBSTITUTE TEACHER
#13: CALLING ALL PLANETS
#14: I'VE GOT A SECRET
#15: HOW TO BE COOL
#16: THE NOT-SO-GREAT OUTDOORS
#17: MY HO-HO-HORRIBLE CHRISTMAS
MY AWESOME HOLIDAY FRIENDSHIP BOOK
(An Activity Book)
FULL HOUSE MICHELLE OMNIBUS EDITION
#18: MY ALMOST PERFECT PLAN
#19: APRIL FOOLS!
#20: MY LIFE IS A THREE-RING CIRCUS
#21: WELCOME TO MY ZOO
#22: THE PROBLEM WITH PEN PALS
#23: MERRY CHRISTMAS, WORLD!
#24: TAP DANCE TROUBLE
MY SUPER SLEEPOVER BOOK
#25: THE FASTEST TURTLE IN THE WEST
#26: THE BABY-SITTING BOSS
#27: THE WISH I WISH I NEVER WISHED
#28: PIGS, PIES, AND PLENTY OF PROBLEMS
#29: IF I WERE PRESIDENT
#30: HOW TO MEET A SUPERSTAR
#31: UNLUCKY IN LUNCH
#32: THERE'S GOLD IN MY BACKYARD!
#33: FIELD DAY FOUL-UP
#34: SMILE AND SAY "WOOF!"
#35: MY YEAR OF FUN BOOK
#36: THE PENGUIN
#37: FOR THE BIRDS
#38: IS THIS FUNNY, OR WHAT?
#39: CAMP HIDE-A-PET

Published by Pocket Books

1033-36

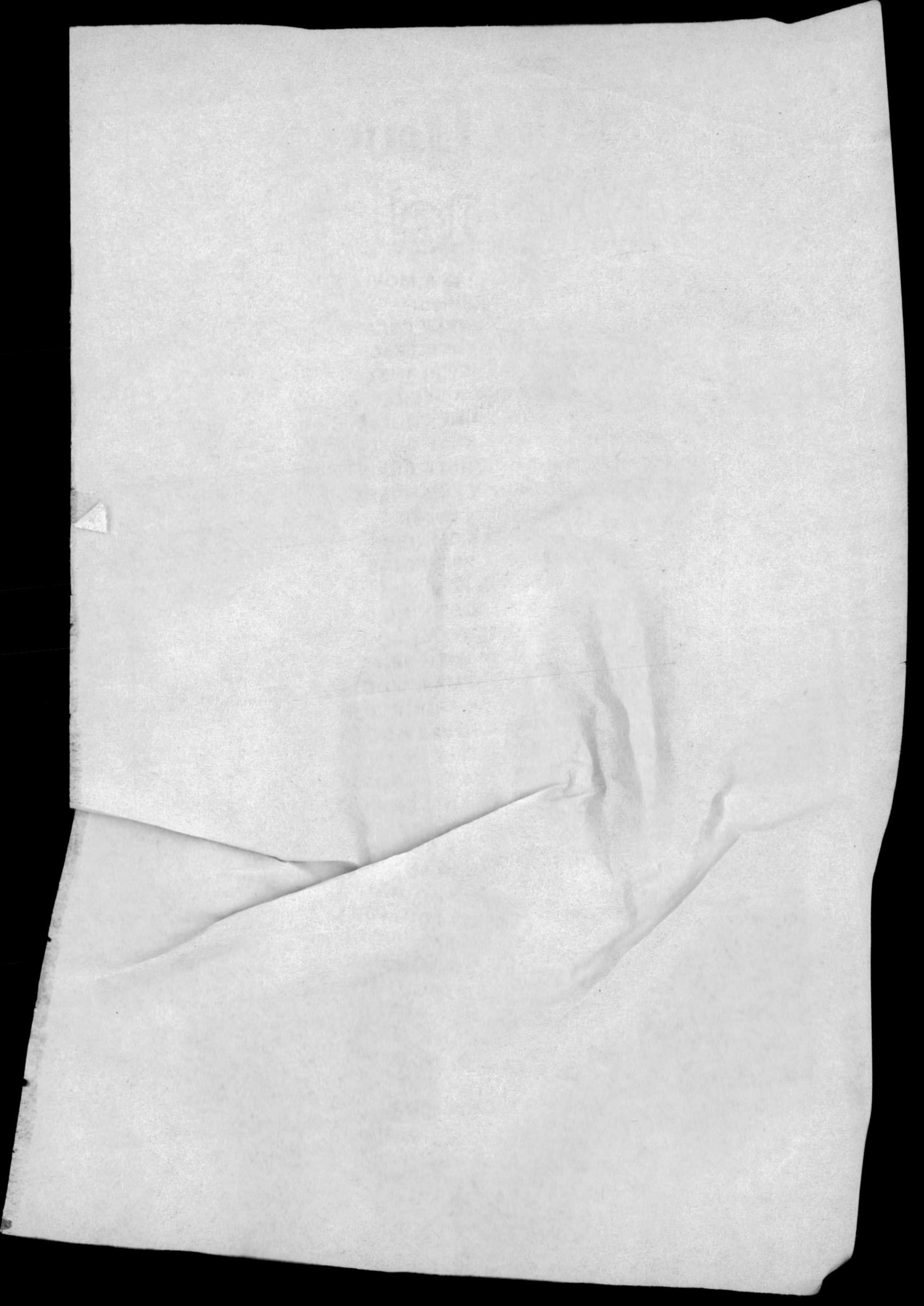

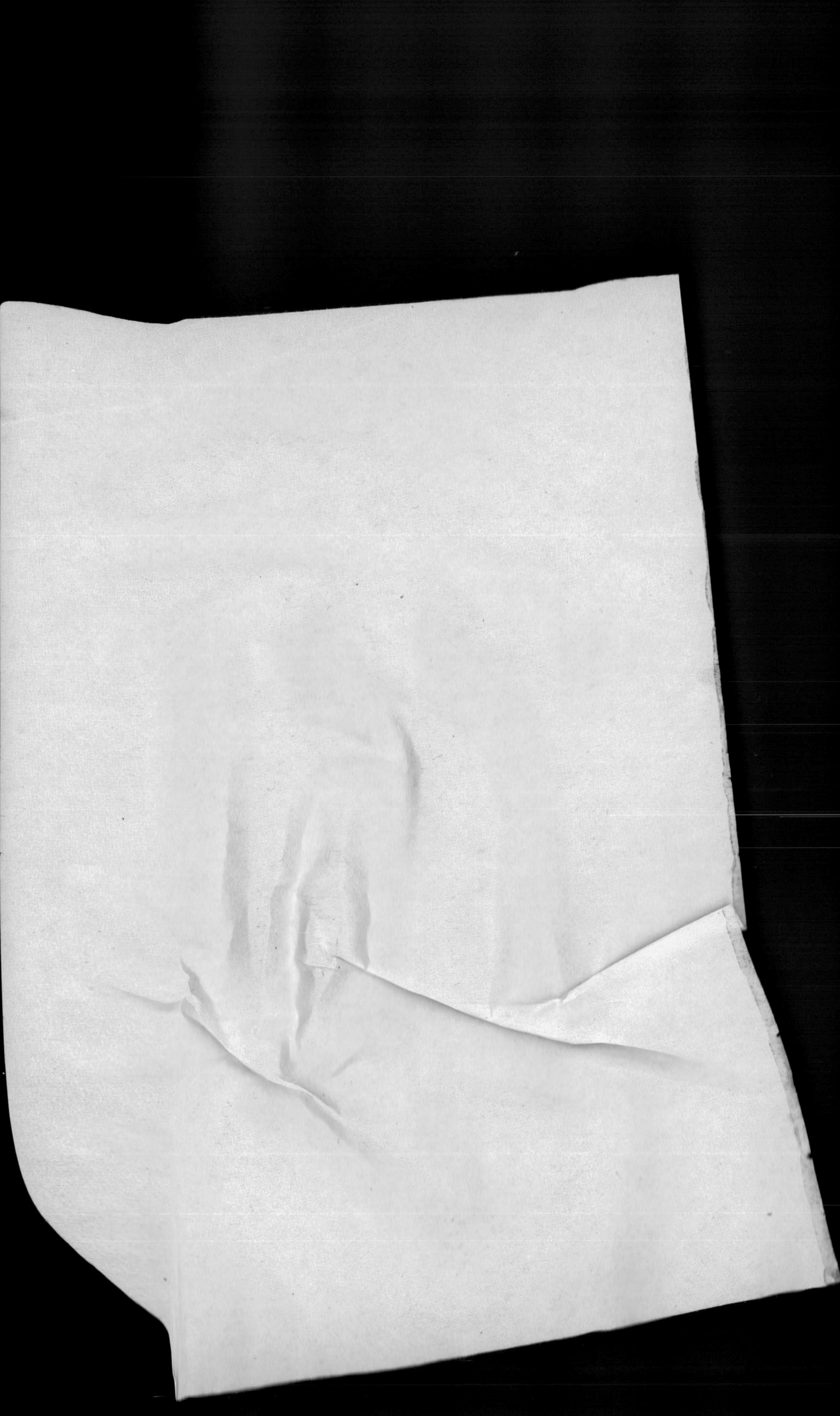